NEVER THE FA

NEVER THE FACE

A Story of Desire

ARIEL SANDS

ST. MARTIN'S PRESS

NEW YORK

NEVER THE FACE. Copyright © 2011 by Ariel Sands. All rights reserved. Printed in the United States of America. For information, contact St. Martin's Press, 175 Fifth Avenue, New York, N.Y. 10010.

www.stmartins.com

Library of Congress Cataloging-in-Publication Data

Sands, Ariel.
     Never the face : a story of desire / Ariel Sands. — 1st ed.
         p.   cm.
     ISBN 978-0-312-56386-8
     1. Sexual dominance and submission—Fiction.   2. Bondage (Sexual behavior)—Fiction.   3. Sadomasochism—Fiction.   I. Title.
     PS3619.A563N48 2011
     813'.6—dc22

                                                              2010042303

First Edition: April 2011

10   9   8   7   6   5   4   3   2   1

For G, with love

NEVER THE FACE

LAST NIGHT I dreamt of David.

It was a new dream.

We were on the deck of a huge ship, looking out at a land of ice and fire. We were dancing.

It had none of the longing of the old dreams. But it had the intensity.

I don't often think of David now. Once in a while he flits through my mind—if I see someone in the street who looks like him, or I find an old photograph, or a book he gave me. As for the dreams—I hadn't had one for ages. For the most part, the past is remote, and the person I was then seems a stranger.

But this morning, he stayed in my mind. And I found myself hurtling back across the years, back to a spring morning in California when I was—

Awake.

TEN

I ROLLED over and looked at the clock. Four A.M.

How strange. Usually, when I've been lying awake for hours, I get angry and restless. My feet kick at the covers. And I twitch from one position to another.

But not tonight.

Tonight, I'm in a state of—well, it's hard to describe. A kind of transcendent calm. Dazed. Still. Relaxed.

And full of wonder.

After a while—perhaps fifteen minutes, perhaps an hour—I stretched, switched on the light, and got out of bed. Chilly. I took the few steps to the end of the room and pulled back the long, pale curtain that hid a tiny cubicle containing a toilet, a sink, and above the sink, a small mirror. The mirror was what I wanted. I shut the lid of the toilet, climbed onto it, pulled down my pajamas, and craned my head to look.

Jesus. Worse than I thought. My buttocks, and the backs of my thighs, were covered in weals. Fat weals. They were already starting to bruise. I ran a finger over one of them. It hurt, a throbbing, twinging echo of the blow that had caused it. I shivered. But not from cold. Was it excitement? Fear? Excitement.

I slid back under the blankets and curled into the warmth. I lay, hovering between sleep and wakefulness, and watched the light start to seep through the slats of the blinds. All of a sudden, I laughed aloud. *He's way ahead of you,* observed a small voice in my head. *You don't often meet a man who makes you feel like an ingénue.*

Again, I heard his voice on the telephone.

"So we're all set for dinner on Thursday," he was saying. "I'll pick you up at seven."

"Great," I said. "I'm looking forward to it."

Then he said, "I'm going to make you bark like a dog."

I giggled. He was always saying things like that. He never meant it.

His voice became hard, full of threat. "I spent the weekend choosing a stick to beat you with," he said.

My heart skipped and thudded.

"Don't be ridiculous, David," I said.

"I'm going to take you to the Gates of Hell and beat you there," he went on.

What is he talking about?

There was an edge to his voice I hadn't heard before. I discovered I was chewing my lower lip.

"What makes you think I'd let you do that?" I said.

"Because I'm an old friend, you trust me, and you know I'll be very rough with you," he said.

Old friend, yes. Trust, yes. Rough? What does that mean?

You know what that means.

A shiver of lust rippled through me.

He can't be serious. He just got married.

Pity.

The flash of disappointment was as raw as it had been six months earlier, when he'd said to me, across a plate of eggs in a crowded café, "Maria and I got married last weekend." I must have looked stricken, because he added, "It was a small ceremony—just family."

I'd smiled, and said, "Congratulations! That's fabulous! I hope you'll be so happy." But part of me was shouting, *No! We'd have been so good together!*

I heard myself saying into the telephone, "But David. What about Maria?"

"She knows about it, and she's okay with it," he said.

What?

For the next two days, my mind argued with itself.

He's teasing. No, he isn't. *He's always made threats, but they've always been empty.* This is different. *Why?* Because this time he means it. This time he's not teasing.

Again and again I heard the menace in his voice as he said, "I spent the weekend choosing a stick to beat you with. . . . I'm going to take you to the Gates of Hell"—*What?*—"and beat you there." Each time, my mind went round the same circle. *He's bluffing.* No. He's not.

Or is he?

I thought of the postcards he'd sent from time to time. "How's my naughty sex kitten? Any good spankings recently?" one had said. "Lashings of love—like switch marks after they've cooled down and you can stare proudly at them in the mirror," said another.

It's all just talk. He's never done anything. Never even tried.

I'm telling you, this time it's different.

It can't be. He just got married.

But if she knows—

I shuddered.

Oh come on, he's teasing. No, he isn't.

And I thought of the dreams I had had about him. The details were different, but the plot was always the same. I was helpless, legs open, waiting. For him. He would come near. My body would begin to tremble with a degree of arousal I had never felt when awake. He would move toward me—about to hit me? About to kiss me?

I never found out. In that moment, I always woke up.

I had never had such dreams about anyone else.

But a dream was one thing. Did I want the reality? Assuming that it was real?

Finally, on Thursday morning, I picked up the telephone. I put it down. *Go on.* I picked it up again, and this time dialed his number. I licked my lips.

Four rings.

A voice. "You've reached David's phone. Please leave a message." *Beep.*

"Hi, David, it's me. I'm afraid something's come up and I won't be able to make dinner tonight. Sorry about this; I'll give you a call later. Bye," I said.

Excellent.

And for the first time in two days, I found I could concentrate on work.

I was in my office, reading dispatches from the Italian trenches, when the phone rang.

"Hello?"

"Come and have dinner with an old friend, and stop your silly freaking out," he said. His voice was warm and reassuring, as if

I'd imagined the previous conversation. "I'll pick you up from your office at seven. Look pretty for me."

Before I could argue, he'd hung up. I looked down and saw I'd scratched the cuticle around my thumbnail so deeply that it was bleeding.

At seven o'clock sharp, he knocked on the door.

"Hi, David, come in, sorry, I'm not quite ready."

"Take your time," he said, giving me a hug. "Nice office."

"Yes, it's great," I said. I pointed at the darkness beyond the window. "You can't see much now, but during the day it has a wonderful view of the hills. How are you?"

"Good," he said, looking out of the window. "Busy. Flying to Japan tomorrow for a business trip. Be away a few days."

I went over to the desk. What did I need? Not much. I picked up a couple of books and put them in my bag. As I did so, I became aware that he was staring at me. A tremor ran through me, and I heard myself talking wildly and irrelevantly about a recent vacation I'd been on. An amused smile flickered on his face, but he said nothing.

We walked together to his car, and got in. I glanced around. The backseat was deep in papers, books, socks, and T-shirts. A Styrofoam box of congealed food lay half open under a tennis racquet.

He saw me looking. "Nothing changes," he said. We both laughed.

"I've booked a restaurant you'll like," he said, putting the keys into the ignition. He started the engine, and pulled into the road. "But we have to make a stop first."

"Where are we going?" I said.

"You'll see."

He drove along a series of small streets, then parked. "Here we are. Get out."

We were in front of an art museum. He opened the trunk of the car, and took out a stick.

"Put this between your teeth. Carry the stick I'm going to beat you with."

"No! David!"

He shrugged, stuck the stick into his belt, grabbed my arm, twisted it behind my back, and propelled me across the street.

"What the fuck are you doing?" I said, struggling.

"Quit it. You're going to get me arrested," he said, his mouth against my ear.

"Good. Damn it, David, let me go." He didn't. I couldn't break free.

We crunched across gravel. We were in the museum's sculpture garden. Up a few steps, and onto a plinth. His grip relaxed. I twisted away, saw a stone bench, and sat on it. And found myself looking at a huge bronze sculpture of writhing figures, their mouths open in infinite screams. For a moment, I didn't recognize it.

Then I realized. *It's the Gates of Hell.*

If I hadn't been so on edge, I would have laughed.

David sat down beside me.

I turned to glare at him. "David—" But I got no further. As I started to speak, he put a piece of chocolate into my mouth. A small piece of expensive dark chocolate. It melted on my tongue, thick and bittersweet. I sat in sudden silence, just tasting.

The evening was cool, but clear; a light breeze was making the leaves of the palm trees rustle. A door in the side of the museum opened. Some people came out. I hoped they would loiter, but they all walked toward the row of parked cars and, one by one, drove away. Nobody disturbed us.

He broke off a piece of chocolate for himself and got to his feet.

"Stand up."

"No."

"Come on, stand up. We'll leave the stick here."

He put the stick on the bench. I glanced at it. About two feet long, it was pale, thin, and slightly bent. It looked light. It looked like a toy.

So he was bluffing.

I stood up. He reached out, put his hand in my hair, and twisted. I yelped, and tried to pull away. I couldn't. His knuckles dug into the back of my head, drawing my hair tight against my scalp. I waved my arms; he wrenched my head back so they flailed the air. He forced my face upward, and kissed me, savagely, roughly. With his free hand, he reached down into my sweater, into my bra, and touched my breasts. Not softly, the way most men will, but with a casual brutality, as if he didn't care whether I liked it or not. Squeezing, pulling, pinching. I squirmed and began to cry out; he clapped his hand over my mouth and nose, his fingers digging into my cheeks. I couldn't breathe. I started to panic.

He let go. I staggered, gasping.

"Let's go to dinner," he said. "You look like you need a drink."

He picked up the stick, and led the way to the car. Too startled to object, I followed.

He started driving.

"Spread your legs," he said.

"No."

He let go of the steering wheel, reached across, took one knee in each hand, and wrenched them apart.

"In my car, that's how you sit. It's okay: you're new to this."

He ran his right hand lightly along the inside of my thigh; despite myself, I felt my body give a responsive shudder. Then, *wham.* He smacked me hard, the flat of his palm against my thigh. I jumped. My thigh smarted.

"What do you say?"

"Ow! What did you do that for?"

He laughed. "Fair enough. But next time I hit you, you say 'thank you.'"

"Don't be ridiculous," I said.

He cocked an eyebrow. "You'll learn."

The museum was a short drive from the downtown strip. David parked at a meter on the side of the street. We were underneath a street lamp; a pool of light fell on my lap as though it was a stage being lit for a play. I bit my lip and glanced at the sidewalk. *I hope no one walks past.*

He turned to me. I thought he was going to kiss me. Instead, he lunged at me, sending his left arm between my open thighs toward my crotch as if he was going to punch me. I leapt backward, flinging myself up the seat.

He didn't touch me. Yet as he reached toward me, a surge of pleasure flooded my groin. The sensation was so powerful that I had to fight to suppress a moan. *No one has made you feel pleasure like that before. And he did it without even touching you.* I stared at him.

He smirked. "Let's get you that drink," he said.

The restaurant was around the corner. It was a convivial, busy place with chunky tables of dark wood, dim lighting, and an open kitchen. As we sat down, David said, "I'll get you a drink you'll like," and ordered two mojitos, one for me, and one for himself.

A what? I'm sure I'd prefer a glass of white wine.

I was wrong. I liked the cold, tropical tang of the mojito.

But—what on earth was going on?

I glanced at him as he studied the menu. He appeared absorbed in it, and gave no sign that the evening was at all peculiar. As he turned the page, his wedding ring glinted. It was broad, hammered gold.

"Seriously, David, what about Maria?" I blurted out.

"I told you: she knows about it, and she's okay with it," he said, looking up.

I stared at him. Maybe I'd gotten him—them—completely wrong. Maybe they did this every other week.

"Do you do this often?" I said.

"Never in ten years."

"Why me? Why now?"

He shrugged.

"I told Maria you were worried about her."

"What did she say?"

He mimicked a snide woman's voice, "'Why does she care?'"

"But David, of course I care, you're one of my oldest friends. If—" My voice cracked and I didn't finish the sentence. *If.*

He nodded, but said nothing. I picked up the mojito and took another sip. He watched me. His face was inscrutable.

The waiter came over. "What can I get you?" he said.

I opened my mouth to answer. But before I could say anything, David said, "My friend will start with asparagus, followed by the quail. I'll have—" but I didn't hear the rest of the sentence. *Hey! He just decided what you're going to eat. He just—told the waiter. How dare he?* I glared at him. Now he was saying, "and bring us a bottle of—" The waiter nodded and went off.

"David—" I said, preparing to object.

He wasn't listening. "The food here is great. You'll love it," he said. As he spoke, I realized something else. *He chose for you what you were about to order anyway. You lived with Sam for three years, but he could never have chosen food for you.* I glanced at David again. *How did he know what you'd want?*

He smiled, and I had the sudden impression he knew what I was thinking. I felt transparent, as though my skull were glass and he could see the thoughts traveling around my brain. I shivered.

But then he launched into a story about some consulting he'd been doing for a shipping company in Korea—"so we went to this wild karaoke bar, I can't sing, but I had to"—and the evening began to feel more normal.

"What did you sing?"

"'Puff, the Magic Dragon.'"

"'Puff, the Magic Dragon'? No. Seriously?"

I had a vision of David on stage, crooning into a microphone, surrounded by Korean businessmen, their ties loose, their faces flushed.

He shrugged. "I had to sing something. It's easier than most songs. And it has a story. It has—"

"A beginning, a middle, and an end," I said. I knew what he liked.

He looked at me and smiled. "Yes. Not like that play we went to in London—three men in a pub telling ghost stories. That had no structure."

He took a piece of bread and reached for the butter. "Speaking of London," he said, "time to eat like the English." He cut a chunk of butter and put it on his plate. Then, instead of buttering the whole piece of bread, he made a great show of spreading a tiny piece of butter onto one corner and then taking a bite, repeating this over and over again until the bread was gone.

We both laughed. I remembered my effete English friend Philip Poppleton claiming that a German spy had been caught during the war because he didn't know that the way an English gentleman eats toast and marmalade was to do exactly what David had just done: to prepare each bite one at a time, not smear the whole slice and then eat it. I'd told David that story—when? *The first time he visited you in London.* Yes. How he'd hooted: "That. Is. Hilarious."

"That still cracks me up," he said, as the waiter came over to pour the wine. "Cheers," said David, raising his glass. "And congratulations on your fellowship."

"Oh, thanks," I said. "Cheers. Mmm. It's delicious." The wine was superb.

"So tell me about this new gig—how does it work?" said David.

"Well, basically, it's three years to do what I want, where I want," I said. "No teaching, just research. The pay isn't great, but it's enough."

"It's fucking prestigious, though," he said. "I read about it."

"Oh—" I said, staring at the table.

"You don't have to play modest with me," he said. "You're first class; you deserve it." I fidgeted. He laughed. "You still need to learn to take compliments, though. But now you're the queen of your own time, what are you going to do with it?"

"The fellowship starts in June. Before that, I've got another two weeks in the archives here, then I go back to London. I'll be there until the end of May." I paused.

"And then?"

"Then I move to Italy."

"Rough life being you," he said. "What's in Italy?"

"I've organized a position at—" and I named an institute. "It's in the north, in a small town near Milan. It's a great place—they provide an apartment, and an office if I want it. I'll mostly be working in the archives; but I also have to improve my Italian, so for the first few months I'll be taking Italian classes." I took a sip of wine. "At the moment, most of the Italian I know is from operas, so I can say 'Repent!' and make long speeches about infidelity. Which doesn't help me much with propaganda in the First World War."

He laughed.

"It's a little scary," I said. "My friend Gio lives in Rome, but that's miles away, and apart from him I don't know anyone in Italy."

"You'll make friends," he said. "You always do. It's one of your gifts." He thought for a moment, then added, "Gio—is he that gay guy you knew in grad school? The one you said used to wear purple shoes?"

"Yes, that's right; we shared an apartment for a few months. He's a sweetheart." I thought of Gio, hair disheveled, purple shoes unlaced, discussing boyfriend trouble, the secret of good risotto, and the joys of listening to jazz while in the bath.

"How are you folks doing?" said the waiter, clearing the plates from the first course. "Everything okay here?"

"Great, thanks," said David.

As the waiter left, I said, "There's something I wanted to ask you."

"Go ahead."

"I've managed to save up a little money, but I don't know what to do with it. My cousin has offered to invest it for me—"

"I hope you're not even considering letting him do that."

I looked at him, abashed. But his expression was thoughtful, not contemptuous as I'd feared.

"You're a successful, independent woman; you need to know how to invest your own money," he said.

"I find it so confusing—"

"You took calculus in college. There's nothing in this you can't handle. You just need to know some basics. Here." He took a pencil and a notecard out of his pocket and began explaining.

As we talked, I forgot about the Gates of Hell and the weirdness and tension of the previous days. But as I was laughing at a joke he'd made, I felt the sudden pressure of his hand on my knee. His touch made me quiver.

"Spread your legs," he said, his voice low.

"Don't be silly. We're in a restaurant."

Again, he raised an eyebrow. As he did, my knees separated of their own accord until I was sitting with my legs splayed open. I felt vulnerable and louche. I blushed. *Thank God the tablecloth is long.*

"Good girl," he said.

I swallowed.

He offered me a piece of his steak, speared on the end of his fork. "Open up," he said, and I found my mouth obeying, opening wide, receiving the mouthful. I wanted to resist, but there was something warm, something pampering about it, that I couldn't say no to. After feeding me one particularly greasy mouthful, he leant over and wiped my lips with his napkin. Again, his wedding ring glinted.

The sight made my stomach clench.

I told you: she knows about it and she's okay with it.

I glanced at him. Is she really "okay with it"?

Does she really not care that I am here, sitting with my legs spread while he feeds me from his plate?

I wish I knew her. I wish I'd met her more than that one time.

I turned to David to ask him more about her, but something about his expression stopped me. Instead, I found myself asking for news of a mutual friend.

When the bill came, I reached for it, but David caught my hand and placed it on the table. He put his credit card on the tray, handed it to the waiter, then looked at me and said, "If you pay, I have to put out."

Despite myself, I laughed. "Do you remember how that used to annoy Rebecca?" I said. In my mind, I saw David sitting across from a tall girl with a long ponytail. He was smiling slightly; her face was pink. "You pig!" she said, her voice a hiss.

He rolled his eyes. "That chick wouldn't let a guy buy her a burger and fries in case he felt entitled to a kiss afterward. I think she thought letting a guy pay for a meal was the same as being a prostitute."

"We were all a bit like that in college," I said.

"All that crap about wanting to be called 'women' instead of 'girls,' but totally missing what really matters. Which is why," he said looking at me, "a successful thirty-three-year-old woman doesn't know how to invest her money." I blushed. "Instead of accusing guys of sexism for trivial bullshit, they should have been setting up investment clubs. So they'd know how to use their equal pay for equal work."

He signed the check, and led the way back to the car.

He began to drive.

"Where are we going?" I said.

"I thought I'd drop you home," he said.

I was overwhelmed by an odd flatness. Was that it? Had he changed his mind? Had I let him down?

Silence. Just the car's engine roaring and subsiding as we came to, and then drove through, stop signs.

We arrived.

"Well, thank you," I said. I unbuckled the seat belt.

He looked at me. "Aren't you going to invite me in?"

He wants to come in? I felt confused. And hot, though the evening air was cool.

"Oh. It's not very grand. It's sort of a glorified garden shed. Actually, it's not that glorified. More of a shack. I'm renting it from a grad student who's gone away for the winter, I think he's on an archaeological dig in Sri Lanka." I'm babbling. Why?

David kept looking at me. "But yes, would you like to come in?" I said.

He opened the trunk of the car and, this time, took out a riding crop. *What? Oh fuck.* I swallowed.

"Let's go," he said.

We tiptoed past the main house and along the garden path to the shed.

"Welcome to the shack," I said, as I switched on the light. It was bright, severe.

He came in, glanced around, shut the door.

"Take off your clothes."

"No."

He shook his head, took me in his arms, and stripped me. He did not undress.

"Get on the bed. On all fours."

I went to turn off the light.

"Leave it."

"Please, David, let me turn off the light."

"No. I want to look at you." He jerked his head. "Get on the bed."

I curled up on the bed, making myself small. Hiding my body as much as I could.

"No, not like that." He uncurled me. "Hands and knees. Let's see pretty dog." He put me on all fours, then put his hand in my hair and pulled. "Head up. Arch your back. Proud bitch."

He gazed at me.

Then he hit me.

Across the buttocks. With the riding crop.

Slamming pain. I yelled, and lurched forward, falling onto my belly. My buttocks burned.

He put his hands on my hips, and pulled me back up. "Pretty dog," he said again, running his hands along my stomach, caressing my breasts. "Show me how strong you are."

I tried not to flinch as he hit me again. And again. And again.

He put his hand between my legs, dipped his fingers into my pussy. He smiled slightly, and took his hand away. "You are such a bitch," he said.

"No, I'm not," I said, offended.

"Yes. You are. Now bark for me. Just a little one."

"No!"

He hit me again, harder. A wave of pain crashed on my leg. I yelled.

"Do it. Bark."

Silence. He leant over and whispered in my ear, "Do as you're told. Don't make me force you. Bark."

Silence. I saw his eyes narrow, his arm rise—

"Ruff," I said.

"Good girl." He smiled.

The riding crop smashed into the other leg.

"No, David, stop, please, stop. I don't like it."

He dipped his fingers back into my pussy, then dragged them across my top lip, smearing it with dampness. "Your body is giving you away," he whispered. I reached my hand down. My thighs were drenched.

I'm not sure how long he beat me that night. Time became

suspended. The world shrank to two people inside a shack: nothing else existed.

Eventually, I dropped forward again. Rather than pulling me back to my knees, he covered my body with blankets, and sat, cradling my head, stroking my hair, caressing my neck. He looked down at me, studying my face, saying nothing. I don't know whether it was tenderness that he felt, but it seemed to me that he held me tenderly, that tenderness radiated from his dark, dark eyes.

I gazed at him. I felt serene, at peace.

Perhaps this is what they mean by "bliss."

After—how long? I don't know—he said, "Are you okay?"

I nodded.

"Are you sure?"

I nodded again.

"I've got to get home. When I've gone, go to the bathroom and admire your welts in the mirror. Play with yourself. I'll call you next week."

He kissed me gently—so gently that I gasped—and vanished. I lay snuggled under the blankets. My body seemed to be floating. My mind was still. I was just there, listening to the noises of the night.

NINE

HE BEAT me on a Thursday. Three days later, he came back.

I was about to go out. I put on my coat, picked up my bag, and opened the door. David was standing on the other side of it, his hand raised ready to knock. I looked at him, and swallowed.

"Where do you think you're going?" he said, advancing on me, pushing me back inside.

"What are you doing here? I thought you were in Japan," I said. Why did my voice sound panicky?

"Trip got canceled. So I thought I'd come and fuck you instead."

He pushed me onto the bed, unzipped his fly, and pulled out his cock. It was hard.

"Suck me," he said.

"Don't be silly," I said. "Come on, David, we can't do this. It's ridiculous."

He shrugged, and sat down on the bed beside me. He put his arms around me and rocked me a little. His arms were strong; I felt small and safe inside them. He smelled of soap and sweat.

A whisper in my ear. "Take off your clothes."

"No, David, quit it, I told you, I don't—"

I stopped. His hands were pulling off my shirt, unfastening my bra. And my body was helping him. Arms went over my head to help him remove the shirt; my back moved so he could better reach the hooks on the bra. A few moments later, I was naked and on all fours. He stood by the bed, fully dressed, his fly still undone.

"Offer yourself," he said.

"What?"

"Offer yourself for fucking," he said.

I stared at him.

"Like this." He took my arms, and moved my hands onto the lower curves of my buttocks. The bruises twinged. I swayed, almost losing my balance and falling on my face.

"Now pull yourself open. Head up, shoulders back, chest out. Arch your back. You're a proud bitch."

The mattress was soft; my position, unstable. I struggled to stay upright. He watched me.

"Good girl. Now, what do you say?"

I said nothing.

"You say, 'Please fuck your bitch.'"

With the involition of someone in a dream, I heard my voice saying, "Please fuck your bitch."

He smiled a small smile—and accepted the invitation. Suddenly, he was naked, kneeling behind me, his hands on my shoulders, his cock pounding inside.

"Beg."

"What?"

"Beg to be fucked."

"Please?"

"Good girl. Again."

"Please."

"Please what?"

"Please fuck your bitch."

"Again."

"Please."

"Again."

"Please."

"I can't hear you."

"Please."

"Louder."

"PLEASE."

"Please what?"

"Please fuck your bitch."

"With each stroke."

"Please-please-please-please-please."

"What are you?"

"Your bitch."

"Is this what you want? Is it? Is it?" He shook me.

"Yes," I whispered.

And it was.

After about an hour, he shuddered and groaned, and we lay together in exhausted silence.

For ten minutes.

He leant over the edge of the bed, reached into his trouser pocket, and took out a shoelace. He tied it around his testicles. *What is he doing? Why does he have a shoelace around his balls?*

As if he hadn't done anything odd, he turned to me and said, "On your knees, Bitch. Offer yourself."

His penis was erect.

So soon?

I began to be scared.

An hour later, I was too tired to kneel. My arms gave way, and I crashed onto my belly. He turned me over—I couldn't stop him—and sat on my face. A smell of musk slammed into my nose.

"Lick my asshole, Bitch," came the command; and as I writhed and gasped for air beneath him, he watched my headless body and jacked off until he came.

He sat on the edge of the bed, undid the shoelace, and looked at his watch.

"Oh shit, I've got to run. We're having some people over for dinner, and I'm going to be late. I'll just jump in the shower and clean up."

"No, you won't. I haven't got one."

"What?"

"I haven't got one. I shower at the gym."

He strode to the end of the room and drew back the curtain of the toilet cubicle. He turned, then looked behind my clothes.

Now it was his turn to be astonished. He looked around, scratched his head, and swore.

He began pulling his clothes on.

"I've got to scram," he said. "I'll take you to dinner on Thursday." And with that he was gone.

I staggered to the sink, and began to wash, submariner style, one piece of my body at a time. I was sponging my breasts when I glanced up and caught sight of my face in the mirror. Hold on. I look different. What is it? Is it the cloud of mussed-up hair? The redness of my lips? No. Then I realized.

I am glowing.

I stared. I had never seen myself look so radiant. All of a sudden, I found I was crying. Smiling, too.

The room was cold. I turned on the tiny heater. After a few

minutes, I turned it off again. It had less oomph than a hairdryer, and was going to make no difference. Instead, I put on pajamas and a sweater, and got into bed.

I thought about the countless times I'd had sex before. They had as much resemblance to what I'd just experienced as a stuffed toy has to a tiger. A small voice pointed out that *tigers are dangerous,* but I ignored it. I was busy, absorbed in recollections and dreams.

My mind drifted through a jumble of images. There I am, sitting in bed, arms around my knees, weeping. Sam is standing by the window, his face riven by hurt. "What do you mean you have a problem with sex?" he said. Anger and misery distorted his voice.

I huddled, hating myself for hurting him so.

"What do you mean? Please tell me," he said.

"I mean I can't respond. I feel like I'm dead." I didn't know I was going to say that. The words came out by themselves. I wished them back, but it was too late. He looked as though someone had knifed him.

"Sex with me makes you feel dead?"

"I'm sorry," I whispered. "I'm so, so sorry."

The scene shifted. We were walking down a beach. "Most women don't reach orgasm during sex," he said.

I glanced at him. What to say? Should I be honest? How would he respond? Would he be shocked? Enthusiastic? Mystified?

I thought of the teasing sparks of pleasure set off by chance encounters—a look, a gesture. *Why can't I get those sensations all the time?*

Why can't I get them from him?

The problem isn't me. It's us.

We walked on. The water eroded the sand from underfoot. Farther down the beach, someone's castle was being washed away.

I imagined myself, naked but for a collar, kneeling before him. He is angry. He is going to punish me. He's going to—

I pushed the images away. Those desires, those dark desires that lurked in the shadows of my mind—most of the time I tried to hide them, even from myself. I had never let myself speak of them.

Tell him. Maybe—

I hesitated.

"Tell me," he said.

"Maybe you should try spanking me," I said.

He laughed.

I bit my lip.

"No, really," I said.

But you'll have to do it as if you mean it. You should punish me for causing you so much misery.

He frowned. "But I love you. I don't want to hurt you," he said.

I sighed. Loudly enough that I broke out of the reverie. I shook my head to dispel the lingering sadness. The room was dark now. Outside, the street was quiet. Should I get up and eat something? No, not hungry. I rolled over, closed my eyes, and found David standing before me, mocking, laughing. And dangerous. Always dangerous.

Dozing. Words jumbling. *Pretty girl . . . Good dog . . .*

I spent the next few days in a state of nervous exhilaration. What should I wear to dinner? I tried on one outfit then another, in the hopes of conjuring something elegant from my wardrobe. After each change, I'd rush to the toilet, climb on the lid, and contort myself in front of the tiny mirror—here's my waist, here's my ankle with this shoe, here it is with that one, does this skirt make me look dumpy?—trying to see the effect. Eventually, I settled on a pair of gray Italian slacks and a tight-fitting black turtleneck sweater. When Thursday evening came, I preened for an hour before David was due to collect me.

Halfway through dinner, he said, "You tried, didn't you? You looked pretty for me. But," he said with obvious relish, "you're not getting any tonight."

I swallowed and tried to hide my confusion. Tried to pretend that I hadn't imagined I might, that I hadn't wanted to spend the evening in his arms.

We were in another restaurant. This time, I hadn't been allowed even to look at the menu: he handed my copy straight back to the waiter. I flushed. Yet, while one part of me raged, another felt coddled and cared for. Which brought a pulse of guilt. *You're not a child. You're not supposed to like this.* I glanced at him; he was watching me, and again I had the sense of being transparent.

He looked happy.

"You were everything I'd hoped you'd be," he said, feeding me a forkful of chicken. "When I beat you, you didn't struggle. You didn't defend yourself."

I was startled to realize that it hadn't occurred to me to try.

"And after I beat you, you wanted to be petted."

I hadn't known I'd wanted to be petted. I hadn't asked; he had just done it.

But if he hadn't? If he had beaten me and then been unkind or indifferent? My mind flinched, horrified at the thought. *Brutality without tenderness.* The phrase went through my mind as though it was a stray line from a poem.

"You are such a bitch," he said.

"No—I'm not," I said, wincing, hating the word. "I wish you wouldn't keep saying that."

He looked at me. He had a small smile on his face. "You don't know what it means, do you?"

"What, 'bitch'?" I said. "Of course I do."

"No. You think it means 'monster'—a woman who acts bad tempered and spiteful."

"That's what it does mean."

He shook his head. "No. Not in sex."

"What is it then?" I said.

He didn't answer immediately. Instead, he studied my face. Then he spoke. "It's what you are at the core," he said. "Someone who wants to surrender, to be taken."

I started to protest. "I—"

He didn't let me finish. "When I told you to get on the bed, you put your arms behind your back with your wrists together. So I could tie you up."

I did? I guess I did.

"In poker, that's known as a tell," he said, his voice quiet.

I shivered.

He fed me another mouthful.

"There was one thing that surprised me," he went on. "You're small. When you take your clothes off—you're really small. I can circle your waist with my hands."

"Why is that a surprise?"

"You have a big personality. You seem bigger than you are."

Good.

I changed the subject. "How was dinner the other night?"

His face took on a distant look. "Uncomfortable. Eating dinner with your wife and her best friends while smelling of another woman's sex—it was uncomfortable."

"Didn't you shower when you got home?"

"No. I was late. When I got in, they were handing out the food."
Then he said, "Maria wanted to know if I made you cry."

She asked? If I cried?

Why would I cry? Pain had sometimes made me howl, or
groan—but cry?

"What did you say?"

"No." The word left a silence in its wake. An expression I couldn't
read flickered in his eyes. Was it disappointment? It seemed to me
that it was.

"But she was happy I made you bark. That made my wife happy,"
he said.

I looked at my plate, trying to hide my face. I wasn't sure I
liked making Maria happy. I found myself wishing she didn't
exist.

He was still talking. "Maria says it's an intimate thing to beat
someone. Way more intimate than fucking," he said.

"Why?" I said, looking up.

"Because it strips away pretense and self-consciousness, it re-
duces you to your essence." I shifted under his gaze. "When you
fuck someone, your mind can be somewhere else," he said. "You
don't have to show anything of yourself. But when you beat someone, or when you are being beaten—you can't help it, you reveal
who you are."

Perhaps I looked skeptical, because he raised an eyebrow and
said, "Think about it. Have you ever fucked a guy you've just met?"

I hesitated. "Yes," I said. "Once."

"If you'd just met a guy, would you let him beat you?"

I thought for a moment. "No." No. It would be impossible.

"It takes trust," he said. "You don't need to trust someone to
fuck them. But to put yourself in someone else's power, to make

yourself that vulnerable—that takes trust." His voice went quiet, as if he was talking to himself and didn't mean to speak aloud. "That's why it brings such closeness."

Closeness. Does he feel it, too? For a moment, I was back in bed, lying in his arms, gazing at his face.

His tone changed. "I hit you harder than I hit her." He sounded pleased.

"Why?"

"That's what she said." He laughed. "Bitch jealousy—" He put on a mocking tone: "'Why won't you hit *me* harder?' Getting all upset because someone else is being punished more."

"Well? Why did you hit me harder?"

He shrugged. "I'll say to you what I said to her: to each according to her needs."

Needs? What does that mean?

Back at the street in front of the shack, we both got out of the car. He hauled my bag out of the trunk. Then he took out the riding crop, and stuck it through the handles of my bag. "Take that in," he said. "We'll need it next time."

So there will be a next time.

He reached into the trunk again, and took out the white stick. The one I'd decided was a toy.

I went to kiss him good night. As I moved toward him, he brought the white stick down across my buttocks.

It was not a toy.

It was a nasty, whippy switch. I lurched, and stifled a yell.

Someone walked past.

David stood in the street, his face in shadow, his posture tight with coiled menace.

I could have run or shouted, but I was mesmerized.

He hit me again, cutting across the backs of my thighs.

Footsteps. Another person walked past. He held the stick behind his back. We stood in silence. I couldn't drag my eyes off his shadowed face.

He hit me again. And once more.

Then he handed me the stick. "Keep it. We'll need that next time, too," he said.

I stood on the sidewalk, thighs and buttocks smarting, my body alive with desire, and watched him drive off.

I walked to the shack, unlocked the door, and turned on the light. I dropped the bag, hesitated for a moment, then picked up the riding crop and the stick. They were about the same length, the same weight. No. The riding crop was heavier. At one end it had a rubber handle, at the other, a triangle of stiff leather. MADE IN ENGLAND said a gold stamp on the triangle. The stick had no handle, no gold stamp. But it flexed easily, and when I flicked it through the air, it made a whooshing sound.

Better hide these. Don't want someone seeing the crop and asking, "Do you ride horses?"

No, I don't. Where shall I put them?

I glanced around. Behind the table? No. Behind the suitcase. Yes, that's good. I can't see them there.

I sat on the bed. Bits of the evening kept replaying themselves in my head. "That made my wife happy . . . made my wife happy . . . Maria wanted to know if I made you cry . . . made you cry, made you cry."

I didn't like it. I didn't like Maria knowing. Asking.

It made me feel as though I was a toy. Their toy. To be played with and then discarded. Or a guinea pig, to be experimented on. *If you hit her, does she cry? No? How can we make her cry?*

As I thought about it, the first—the only—time I had met her began to seem sinister. It began to seem less like a social dinner to meet the wife of an old friend and more like a kind of interview, for her to inspect me, then give—or withhold—her consent.

Again, I saw her coming into the restaurant. She was beautiful, elegant, graceful, soignée. Her hair hung in perfect ringlets around her face; her clothes were tailored. I felt scruffy and clumsy beside her, suddenly aware that my clothes were baggy, my hair, a mess. And I was struck by how different we looked. My hair was so fair it was almost white; hers was black. My skin was pale; hers, tanned. My eyes were blue; hers were dark, darker even than David's. She looked exotic, like an Arabian princess.

As we shook hands, she smiled at me and said, "I've heard so much about you."

I had looked at her in surprise. *Really? I know hardly anything about you.*

What did I know?

David's voice echoed from the past.

"Maria likes opera; I prefer the theater."

"Maria has a shoe fetish. I want to get her some while I'm here. Maybe a pair of those sexy Italian shoes."

"Maria loves tiramisu."

And, "She married her first husband right after high school, she has a young daughter." *What's the daughter's name again?* Nina. *That's right. She must be in college by now.*

That's it. That's all I know.

No, it's not. There's one more thing.

"The first time I beat Maria, she got up and admired her welts in the mirror. It was screamingly sexy."

When did he tell me that? God, it was years ago—in that

diner around the corner from his first apartment. Remember the twinge of envy? *Remember the thrill of lust?*

For a moment, I saw myself sitting in a booth of a dingy restaurant. I'm holding a cup of coffee; the remains of a waffle sit on a plate in front of me. David is across from me, drinking orange juice.

You—beat her? I didn't know anyone actually did those things.

He looked into your eyes as you were thinking that. Did he see your desire? Was it then, that he knew?

Though I was still wearing my coat, I shivered. And not just because the night was cold.

Again, I heard him saying to me, *Admire your welts in the mirror.* Now I realized it had been inspired by Maria, by their first night together.

And now I started thinking about it, it struck me as odd that I hadn't met her before.

Yes, they'd only been married for six months, but they'd been together for ten years: there had been plenty of opportunities for us to meet. Each time I'd been in town, I'd invited them to join me for a meal. But she had never come. There was always some excuse. She had to work late. Her mother was visiting. She had a cold. So David and I had always gone out alone.

It's almost as though he didn't want you to meet her. As though he was deliberately keeping you apart.

Until that dinner three weeks ago.

And now, "Maria wanted to know if I made you cry." Again, the words echoed. Made you cry . . . made you cry.

Someone is going to get hurt—and it's probably going to be you.

No. It's not going to be me. I'm not going to let it happen. I'm not going to fall under his spell.

I closed my mind to how badly I already wanted to be with him.

As I took off my clothes and brushed my teeth, I wondered about Maria. Did she find it arousing for her husband to fuck another woman, and then come back and tell her about it? Did she thrill as he teased and titillated her, whispering in her ear about beating me, as he made love to her?

Or was it emotional torture, sadistic and cruel?

I climbed into bed and surrendered myself to dark dreams, dreams I didn't like to acknowledge even to myself. *I am chained up, spread-eagled. But my lover is ignoring me. Another woman kneels in front of him, and he is fondling her breasts, he is about to—*

I pulled my mind back. Even if Maria did have fantasies like that, how could she bear to act them out?

She must be strong.

Or nuts.

I felt as if I was cradling a bomb that at any moment might explode and blow my head off. I pulled the blankets tight around my body.

Friday, Saturday . . . I counted the days on my fingers. Ten days. I'm going back to Europe in ten days. Then I'll be out of reach of this lunacy. *Keep a low profile until then.*

Yes. That's what I'll do. I'll vanish.

I set the alarm for the morning and turned off the light.

EIGHT

FRIDAY. I spent the day working in the archives, out of reach of the telephone and, I hoped, David.

Nothing. Nine days to go.

Saturday. I was working in my office after lunch, when David burst in. He'd been running. He smelled of sweat.

He smelled sexy.

He didn't say hello. He said, "I'm going to beat you tomorrow at two."

"No, you won't," I said. "I promised Gail I'd watch her play soccer."

He stared at me. "You're going to watch your lesbian friend play in a women's soccer match?"

"Yes."

"Can't you cancel?"

"No."

For a second, his eyes narrowed. Then he shrugged. He came toward me, twisted his hand in my hair, forced my face upward, and kissed me. The kiss was rough, violent. He bit my lip. My cheeks felt the scratch of the stubble from his chin. Then he was gone.

Trying to ignore how aroused I was, I turned back to my books.

Sunday. I woke early. Something prompted me not to linger: Was it the sun and the birds? The growling of my stomach? Or the premonition of the hunted? I dressed, and went to get breakfast and do some reading in a café. Which meant that when David arrived at the shack at eight, I was not there.

When I got back I found a note pinned to the door. *Bitch, you missed a morning of the most violent sex,* it said. *I was going to teach you what it means to scream.*

I have it still—I came across it the other day, folded inside an old book. The edges are tattered, the ink, faded. But the scrappy handwriting sent a chill of fear across the years, and for a second I was in front of the shack on a crisp afternoon in early March, glancing around as if he might at any moment appear and force me to my knees.

As I took the note off the door, I shuddered at the ferocity of it. What sort of man is he?

You'll be gone in a week.

Monday morning. Working in my office. Silence.

Monday afternoon. The phone rang.

My mouth went dry. Should I answer? No.

But my hand reached out and lifted the receiver.

"Hello?"

"Bitch, get back to the shack. I'll be there in twenty minutes. I'm going to fuck you with such violence you'll never forget it." I cringed at the greed in his voice.

"But—" I said.

"Do it."

"I'm in the middle of something."

Silence. Waiting. Both of us.

I heard myself say, "I'll see you in twenty minutes."

What? It's the middle of the afternoon. You're working. What are you doing?

"Good girl," he said.

You're crazy.

I know.

While my mind argued, my body left the office, got onto a bicycle, and sped off. I felt as though I was being pulled by a magnet. I was there when he arrived.

"Take off your clothes. Show me pretty dog."

Was it the darkness of his eyes that compelled me to obey? Or the force that emanated from the sneer of his mouth, the set of his jaw, the savage grace of his movements?

As I knelt, naked, on the bed, watching him, I had never been more aware. Of the air on my body, on my nipples. Of sounds from the street. Of a male presence near me, but not touching.

He looked around. "Where are they?"

"What?"

"Don't play dumb. The stick and the riding crop."

I shrugged.

"Well, in that case, I'll have to use a coat hanger," he said, and started to take one off the rack.

"Behind the suitcase," I said.

"Wise choice, Bitch. I didn't want to have to beat you with a coat hanger. They're pretty brutal."

He came up behind me.

"I'm going to give you ten strokes on each thigh."

"No!"

"Yes."

"Hold that." He put the stick in my mouth, sideways, so I looked like a prisoner biting the bar of a cage.

"There. That reminds me I have a choice of things to hit you with," he said.

But was that his reason? Or was it kindness? For he gave me something to bite, and biting, I discovered, eases the need to scream.

The blows were so fast they merged into one. Somehow that diluted the pain, as though the nerves didn't have time to send more than one yell to the brain.

"And here's your treat," he said, plunging his thumb deep, deep inside.

I hear myself moan. I feel myself tremble.

Nothing has ever felt like that before.

I turned my head and gazed at him. He was standing by the bed, pulling his shirt out of his pants.

He began to unbuckle his belt.

I swallowed. "No, David, please."

"Is this what you want? Is it?" he said, pulling the belt free of his pants.

"No, no, please don't."

He folded the belt into a loop, holding tongue and buckle together in his hand and, with casual cruelty, hit me with it, once, twice, across the buttocks.

The oddest thing happened. I was consumed with joy. I quivered, and heard myself let out a small, shuddering moan of desire. I stared at him.

He smiled.

With one "Offer yourself," he was behind me, cupping my

breasts, shaking my shoulders, shouting instructions, and striking me with the riding crop.

He turned me over so I was lying on my back, but this was no missionary position. He was kneeling between my legs.

Suddenly self-conscious, I put my hands over my shaking breasts.

"Bitch, move your hands. I want to see your tits move. If you don't move your hands, I'll beat your tits."

My hands slipped back onto the sheets, leaving my chest bare to his gaze.

His face—fascinated, hypnotized, I watched his face. I saw intense concentration.

I swallowed.

"Grab your ankles and spread your legs. I'm going to give ten strokes to each of your inner thighs."

"No!" I shouted.

"Yes," he said, as he put the riding crop down beside him, and picked up the stick.

The stick—it bites and stings. And inner thighs are delicate. He fucked me as he beat me, and as he beat me, he counted.

I yelled and yelled and yelled.

"Is this how you train a bitch?"

"It looks like it," I said.

The next blow was so savage that I couldn't control my leg: it jerked away, my ankle wrenching itself from my hand. A howl burst from my mouth, filling the room.

"That one doesn't count," he said, grabbing my leg, and returning it upright.

"*What?*"

"It doesn't count."

But that was so unfair. I began to cry.

He paid no attention.

As he shook me, and ordered me to beg for more, I began to feel as though my body belonged to him, not to me.

I lay, sobbing; he knelt, fucking me and beating me, not stopping at ten, no longer counting, not heeding my screams.

His face convulsed as he cried out.

Silence.

He picked up his shirt, and used it to dry my face. He kissed my neck, my ears, my nipples, the insides of my elbows, the backs of my knees. He kissed the welts he had made.

"Now you know the meaning of 'ravished,'" he whispered, running his fingers up and down my back so lightly that I trembled and sighed.

My mind was still. Empty. Again, I had the sensation that my body was floating.

I curled against him, aware of the warmth of his chest, the heaviness of his arms, the scratchy stubble on his chin.

Aware of the sheets, and the twilight.

Just aware.

"I'll drop you at the gym so you can clean up," he said.

We walked out to the car.

"One thing I meant to say," he said. "Can I ask you not to fuck other guys while we're doing this? While I'm fucking two women." He put his hand on the back of my neck and squeezed.

Fucking two women. When he said it, his voice was jubilant. As though this was something he'd dreamt of his whole life.

"You mean, until the end of this week?" I said.

"You think we can go on doing this for the next twenty years," he said, laughing. "Yes, until the end of this week."

We got into the car. "It takes a lot to turn off your internal monologue, doesn't it?" he said.

"Yes." I glanced at him. "How can you tell?"

"Because I'd been beating the crap out of you, but when I asked, 'Is this how you train a bitch,' you still gave a smart-ass reply."

Interesting. Maybe there was more care, more thought, in this than I realized.

As I got out of the car, he took my hand, and looking up at me, kissed it with a gentleness that gave me goose bumps.

How can you resist him now?

The next day, I went for a run with Gail. She saw my legs. Saw the black stripes running up the insides of my thighs, the irregular black splotches on the outsides.

"My God, what happened to you? How did you get those bruises?"

"I had a near miss on a bike," I said. "I didn't come off, but the saddle mashed me up a bit." *You battered woman, you. Inventing excuses.*

"Do you have a vitamin deficiency? Maybe you should go to the doctor," she said.

David laughed when I told him. "Some bitches take aspirin before a beating to make themselves bruise more," he said. *They do?* Then he said, "You should have told her what really happened."

You want people to know?

Thursday morning, early, there was a knock on the door. I was just waking. Disheveled, eyes full of sleep, I surfaced from beneath my stack of blankets, and opened the door.

He came in. "Show me your legs."

I pulled down my pajamas. The bruises were even more lurid than the day before, a mass of purple, green, and yellow. He looked at them, caressed them with his fingers. The touch was light, like a gust of air; but still they twinged. I winced.

"So pretty," he said. *How can he think bruises are pretty?* Then, "We'll let those heal up a bit. Today I'm gonna give my bitch a treat. Get back into bed."

I got in; still dressed, he got in beside me and put his arms around me.

"Play with yourself. I'm going to teach you to come on command."

"What?"

"When you want to come, you beg. You do not come without permission. When I decide you can come, I count backward from ten. If you come too soon, I beat you. If you don't come when I tell you, we stop."

This is never going to work.

But obediently, I reached down. David watched.

It was difficult with an audience. But some minutes later, familiar flickers of pleasure started to rise under my hand.

"Please," I said.

"Please, what?"

"Please, can I come?"

"No."

I took my hand away.

"Don't stop what you're doing."

I put my hand back, lightened the touch, let the flickers die down. This is ludicrous.

Then a few minutes later, again, "Please."

"No."

Then, "Ten."

Now I'm nowhere close. This is hopeless.

"Nine. Eight. Seven."

This is absurd.

"Six. Five. Four. Three."

Spasms starting. Incredible.

"Two. One. Come, Bitch, come now!"

I did.

It worked. How—?

I looked up into his face. His eyes were half closed.

"Good girl," he whispered, as he cuddled me, stroked my hair.

"From now on, you want to come, you ask. I control your pleasure as well as your pain."

I lay there, relaxed and surprised.

Saturday morning. Hungry. And scared.

Get out of here. Now.

I pulled on my jeans, wriggled into my sweater, grabbed my
coat, and opened the door.

Too late.

He was there.

"Where do you think you're going?" He came in, closed the
door. "Take off your clothes, Bitch."

"David, please be gentle. Please."

He smiled, and handed me a compact disc. "You'd better put
the music on."

Music. So no one will hear me scream.

I put the disc into the stereo and hit PLAY.

Primeval chantings swirled, reverberating through the room.

"Get on your knees. Let's see pretty dog," said David. Once again I knelt naked on all fours on the bed. The air was cold.

David took four thin leather straps out of his pocket. Each fastened with a buckle. Each was decorated with a small steel chain, and had a steel ring where a shackle could be attached.

He put one of these around each of my wrists and each of my ankles. He then produced two carabineer clips, using one to shackle my ankles together, the other, my hands.

For a moment, he stood and looked at me. Then he reached into his pocket again, and pulled out a long metal chain. It was one of those strangle leashes for a dog, the kind that gets tighter if the animal pulls away. He slipped it around my neck. The metal was heavy and cold on my skin.

He was still dressed.

He blindfolded me.

And went behind me.

I felt his hand on my thighs, tracing out the bruises.

"Please, David."

"I'm careful," he said.

He started to beat my buttocks with the stick. I yelled, my voice vanishing in the din.

"What are you?"

"Your bitch."

"Bark."

"No."

A pause.

"What?" he said, quietly, his voice angry.

"Ruff."

He pushed something—something large—roughly into my pussy.

Something—"NO!" I yelled as he tried to push something else into my asshole. A different pain from the beating: an acute, searing pain. I struggled to escape.

"Sit!"

I stopped.

More searing pain. I screamed. He stopped.

Then he said, "I'll be back in an hour."

No! What if my landlady comes by and finds me kneeling naked on the bed, trussed up and skewered on a dildo?

"No, David, no please. Don't leave me here with the door unlocked. Please. Please."

I struggled, and managed to pull down the blindfold.

He was by the door.

He stared at me.

"Bad dog," he whispered.

He walked toward me. I licked my lips. My body was taut, aware.

"No, please," I said.

He shook his head.

"No, David, please."

He took my left breast in his hand.

He looked at it for a moment, then brought the stick down onto it, hard. And again. And once more, this time across the nipple.

The welts came up immediately. Scarlet stripes on pale skin.

I began to cry. "Please. Please don't leave the door unlocked. And I'm cold."

"Next time, I beat your pussy."

He tied the blindfold on again, tied the leash to my ankles—now I couldn't move without the leash tightening round my neck—and threw a blanket over me. I heard him go out and close the door.

I heard the key turn in the lock.

Soaring voices filled the shack: the music was becoming dramatic, apocalyptic.

Shivering.

I heard his voice, speaking from the past, from years ago. He was telling me a story about a woman he knew.

"They're having anal sex, and her boyfriend says, 'Come on, can't you at least pretend it hurts? I'd enjoy it more if you screamed.'"

I thought about the only time I'd tried to have anal sex. It had been with my college boyfriend, Bobby. I had shrieked, and he'd stopped immediately.

David isn't going to stop.

It's going to hurt. It's going to really hurt.

Concentrate on the music.

The music. He's forgotten to turn it off.

The thought sent a splash of comfort: I realized that the music gave me a way to measure time.

Muscles starting to shake. I shifted, and felt the leash closing, tighter, tighter on my neck. *Fuck.* He can't leave me here for an hour.

He didn't.

The music had only moved on three tracks when I heard the door being unlocked again.

I sensed him crossing the room, kneeling on the floor beside me.

"Open up," he said.

I opened my mouth. He filled it with something cold, soft, and sweet.

Jelly. He is feeding me jelly. He stroked my hair.

He got up. I heard him unzip his pants.

The bed sank as he knelt behind me. He ran a thumb down

my spine, then leant over me and whispered in my ear: "No one has taken your asshole?"

"No."

"No? You're sure?"

"Bobby and I tried once, but it hurt too much, so he stopped."

"What, that skinny red-headed guy you went out with all through college?"

"He wasn't skinny. He was lean." I thought of Bobby, his face in a big smile, talking about rock climbing and how to bivouac on a cliff face.

David laughed. "Sweet of you to defend him; I like a girl who'll speak up for an ex while she's tied up, blindfolded, and has a dildo inside her. Wish he could see you now." His voice became a hiss. "You'd still be with him if he'd had the balls to fuck you anyway, to take you through your tears. If he'd had the balls to own you."

Was that true? *Probably.* I shivered.

A pause. "What about Sam?"

"We never tried," I said.

He undid the blindfold, kissed my neck, and rubbed his finger against my asshole.

"Those nice boyfriends of yours—they left this hole for me." His voice was sneering, gloating, marveling.

"No, please," I said.

He pulled the dildo from my pussy. It was thick, purple, and bulbous. "This is purple jack," he said, waving it. He gestured to a long, black, penis-shaped dildo lying on the bed. "That's black jack. You got on better with purple jack, just so you know."

He slid himself in where purple jack had been, whetting his appetite, wetting his penis. A couple of thrusts, no more. Then pressure on my anus, and tearing, ripping, blinding pain. I yelled, and leapt forward, arching up and away from him.

"Don't fight me," he whispered.

I forced my body to relax. He had his hands on my hips, driving me onto him. I am screaming. The music is screaming. The only thing that exists is searing, screaming pain.

A few moments later, he gave out a shuddering groan, and it was over.

I am whimpering.

"What do you say?"

Silence. My brain won't function.

"Bitch, what do you say?" he hissed.

"Thank you?" I said.

"No. You say, 'David, you forgot to use my mouth.'"

He pulled out. I collapsed, sprawling and devastated, on the bed. *Cuddle me. Please cuddle me.*

"Get dressed," he said. He unshackled my wrists and ankles, but left the leash around my neck. "We're going to the city. And you're going to wear the leash in public."

I didn't protest. There was no point: I would lose. Anyway, I was in no state to argue: My mind was blank. I stumbled over to the rack where my clothes were hanging. I needed to do laundry. I had nothing suitable. I picked out a pair of black trousers, and a black turtleneck sweater. He stopped me from putting on the turtleneck. "I want everyone to see the leash," he said. "I want everyone to know what you are."

I swallowed, and put on my only clean shirt. It didn't match the pants. The choker sat heavily on my neck; the chain hung down my back, cold against my skin. Apparently he didn't expect to hold the other end of the leash: that was something. Perhaps people would just think I was wearing an unusually chunky necklace.

"Where are we going?" I put on my coat.

"I'm taking you to brunch."

By the time we got to San Francisco and found somewhere to park, I was wobbly. My body hurt. The choker was heavy. And I was very, very hungry.

Finally, we were at a table and food was in front of us. Dim sum. Rich smells of garlic and ginger, cooked meats, and roasted fish reached my nostrils. *It smells delicious.*

But I was starting to sway. My eyes were filling with darkness. The preludes to passing out.

As if through a thick foam, I heard David say, "Are you all right?"

I didn't reply: I was struggling not to faint. David said again, urgently now, "Are you all right?"

"Yes," I said, as the feeling passed. I pulled at the choker.

"You can take that off," he said.

I went into the bathroom, and lifted the chain off my neck. My shoulders straightened, the tension in my neck eased. I returned to the table and handed the chain to David. As he took it from me, he smiled a warm, gentle smile, and kissed my hand. Suddenly I felt cherished. Like a precious possession.

We gorged on pot stickers, spring rolls, crispy duck, soft white buns filled with meat, chicken wrapped in foil, and more. Sometimes he said, "Open up," and fed me with his fingers. I began to feel better.

He was laughing. "I was supposed to play tennis last night, but when I got to the court I found that one of my shoes was missing a shoelace. I'd grabbed it in a hurry and forgotten to put it back."

"Why do you use the shoelace?" I said. "What does it do?"

He raised an eyebrow.

"When I was a kid, I started experimenting with sensation. Tying something around my balls makes it easier for me to come— particularly a second or third time."

"Doesn't it hurt?"

"Not unless you forget to take it off."

It was a beautiful afternoon: blue sky, a light breeze. Arm in arm, we went for a walk along the water, laughing, talking. I pointed across the bay at the docks on the far side, at the big cranes, the ones that look like giant metal horses.

"I love those," I said.

Farther on we came to a street market. He looked around. "This is what I like," he said. "Transactions. Commerce."

His voice took on a faraway sound. "It's sexy to pay for sex," he said.

"Have you ever been to a prostitute?"

"No."

How can one word contain so much regret and thwarted desire?

"I've often thought what I could do in a business meeting with a naked bitch on all fours," he said. A pause. Then, "I entertain business guys in strip clubs sometimes. But it's a little vulgar."

I stared at him. I thought of the men sitting together, watching naked girls. Wanting to fuck them. And I thought of how I wasn't supposed to approve of strip clubs, or the men who went to them.

We got back into the car.

"Don't make me tell you again," he said.

"What?"

He nodded at my knees. His nod had the force of an open sesame—again, of their own accord, my knees separated, and I was sitting with my legs spread.

"Good girl."

"Where are we going?" I said.

"I'm going to take you back and fuck you some more."

Something didn't make sense. I had the odd feeling that something had been left out of the excursion: it seemed to me we'd come a long way to have breakfast and a stroll around a market. But perhaps I was imagining it.

Just before we swung onto the freeway, he pointed at a door we were passing. "That's Stormy Leather. That's where I bought the riding crop and the stick. Best fetish shop in San Francisco. Caters too much to the Halloween-Every-Day crowd—but I guess it has to."

"The Halloween-Every-Day crowd?"

He laughed. "Yes. The ones who think rough sex is all about dressing up in silly costumes—hoods and capes and gimp masks. This city's full of them. You can see them at the Power Exchange on the weekends, holding slave auctions."

You can?

His voice became scoffing. "They're the pussies who use safe words when they 'play.'"

"What's a safe word?" I said.

"It's a way to say"—he put on a whine—"'Oh! Stop what you're doing, I can't take it.'" He paused. "Safe words—it's like someone telling you to wear a seat belt and a crash helmet during sex. Kinda takes the edge off." He changed gear and passed the car ahead of us. "A good top—he knows where his bitch is. He knows what she can take and what she can't. Better than she does herself."

I looked at him. Again, I felt him smearing my top lip with dampness, heard him whisper, "Your body is giving you away." Again, I felt his thumb plunge deep inside. I shifted in the seat.

"David?"

"Yes, my little sex kitten?"

"How did you learn to do all this?"

Silence.

"What I found is," he said, "women like it best when they don't know if they're going to be hit or kissed."

"Do a lot of women like being hit?" I said.

"Ask your girlfriends," he said. He glanced at me. "But be careful when you talk about it. People either get this shit immediately or they look at you like you're nuts." He was silent for a moment. Then he said, "Most women are bitches. Not all—but most."

Is that true? I wondered.

He was still talking. "I remember reading a good quote somewhere—can't remember who said it. It went: 'Some women respond to the whip, and some to the kiss. Most like a mix of both.'" He looked at me with his eyes narrowed. "In my experience, that's about right," he said.

"Have you ever been with someone who didn't like it?" I said.

"Once. Remember Ashley?"

I did. She was one of those thin women—tiny breasts and skinny arms—who look great in anything. I thought of her as I'd last seen her: on David's arm, coming into the ballroom of a big hotel. There she is: all legs and black stockings, and the V of her dress comes down to her navel. *Wish I could I wear that.* "Congratulations to the graduating class of —— University," says the disc jockey; the crowd screams and cheers. Loud music, flashing lights. Everyone else is jiggling up and down, but she and David are dancing with sinuous grace. Together, they are lewd, lascivious. I watch, envious and aroused. *Why can't Bobby dance like that?*

"Look at that guy," says Bobby, nodding at David, whose hands were grinding Ashley's hips into his. "How crass."

"Yes," I said, wishing it was me in a skimpy dress being pressed against David's pelvis.

"I remember Ashley," I said, keeping my eyes on the highway.

"She didn't respond to any of this stuff. She wanted to talk about her day."

"During sex?"

"Yeah."

I had a vision of Ashley, with her bobbed hair, her skinny legs and skinny arms, fucking David, talking about the grades she'd got in economics class. *"And then the professor—oh yes, oh God—then the professor handed out the papers—"*

"That must have been difficult for you," I said.

"It was."

I thought of the stick crashing onto my thigh.

"But I wouldn't say I like being hit," I said.

"No one does," he said. "This has nothing to do with liking pain. If you liked pain, you wouldn't ask for Novocain when you go to the dentist." He looked at me. "What you like is knowing I'll hit you," he said.

Yes. Why?

"And you need to be hit. Your body responds to it," he said. *He is smearing my lip with dampness.* "Pain quiets your mind and opens you to pleasure."

Pleasure. I watched him as he drove. Yes, he had brought me more pleasure than any man ever had before.

You only have a few more hours to be with him.

My rib cage felt too small.

"David?"

"Yes?" he said with a smile.

"Why does it work?"

"What? Pain?"

"Yes."

He shrugged. "One. It stops you thinking. Two. Done properly—

not too much, not too little—a beating induces bliss all by it-self."

"Why?"

"Same reason you feel good after running. Your body releases chemicals that give you a high." He laughed. "Why do you think those early Christians used to flog themselves? It took them closer to paradise."

He went on, "I read the other day that the Russians recom-mend beating as a cure for depression."

"Maybe that's all their healthcare system can afford," I said. "It's got to be cheaper than drugs." I pictured a burly Russian writ-ing a prescription, 15 BLOWS TO EACH BUTTOCK EVERY MORNING. TO BE TAKEN AFTER BREAKFAST.

"Maybe. Or maybe they're right," he said. "One time my friend Sarah came to see me. She was in a pissy mood, complaining and whining. I got my riding crop, held her down, and thrashed her. I said, 'You don't come to my place in that sort of mood, you under-stand?' After I was done, she said, 'Thanks, David, I needed that.'"

I stared at him. His eyes were on the road.

Silence.

After a few minutes I said, "David?"

"Yeah?"

"Why do you like making me cry?"

"You're full of questions today." He laughed. "It's not that I like making you cry. It's that when you cry, I know I've got you. I know you're completely present, a body reacting and responding. You're not thinking about anything, or worrying: you're just there."

Silence. The road was empty and he was driving fast.

"I like feeling that I'm with someone selfish," I said.

He looked at me, his face in a half smile. "Kitten, bitches are lazy, selfish, and greedy."

Me? Lazy, selfish, and greedy? No.

Or—am I?

Perhaps I am. Perhaps—perhaps, despite all his rhetoric, all his commands, he is the generous one. *Who is really serving whom?* I began to see glimmers of a paradox.

We turned off the freeway and wound through a series of back roads. He waved an arm. "The property is up there—in those hills. I bought it last summer, just before Maria and I got married."

"Aren't we stopping?" I said.

"No." His face was closed.

"I'd love to see it," I said.

Silence.

Then he said, "Maria said, 'One bitch in the den at a time, David.'"

One at a time.

"You mean—" I said.

He glanced at me, then back at the road. "Yeah, I wanted to fuck Maria while you lick my asshole—or the other way around."

I am chained up, spread-eagled. But my lover is ignoring me. Another woman kneels in front of him, and he is fondling her breasts, he is about to—

I felt myself flush, felt my pussy, my wide-open pussy, ache for his touch.

He cocked his eyebrow and said, "Look how fired up you are."

Back at the shack he didn't need to tell me to beg.

"Please."

"Please what?"

"Please fuck your bitch. Please."

As he fucked me, he said, "Where will I be later tonight?"

"At home."

"That's right. I'll be fucking my wife. Where will you be?"

"Here."

"Alone."

I closed my mind to the cruelty of that. I didn't want to think about it.

Later. "I'll drop you at the showers. You smell like you've been fucked all day."

The beautiful day had turned into a cool, clear evening; a thin moon hung in the sky. I walked back from the showers, breathing in the dry, pungent scent of the eucalyptus. The air seemed tinged with melancholy. It wasn't the echo of David's words, "I'll be fucking my wife. You'll be alone." It was the thought of leaving.

I don't want to go.

I smiled to myself. *You only spent a few hours with him. Maybe not more than eight. You haven't even spent a night together.* Yes, but what hours! I felt a surge of gratitude toward Maria. If, in that moment, she had appeared before me, I would have knelt down and kissed her feet.

You'll never meet another man like him. No. Probably not.

I sat on a bench to postpone the moment I'd have to start packing my suitcase.

The next morning, he took me to the airport.

We got into the car. He reached over and kissed me. He glanced at my legs.

They were already spread.

He smiled a crooked smile. "Good girl."

He started the engine. "Last night, I was this close," he said, gesturing with his thumb and forefinger together, "to coming to get you to sleep at the end of my bed. Where you belong."

But despite the ferocity of his voice, I knew it was bluster: I was leaving, after all. I shrugged. "Too bad," I said.

"Yes."

A few minutes later, he said, "When I get you to the airport, we've got to go back to the way things were." He paused. "Otherwise, I'm going to jeopardize my marriage."

Back to the way things were. I looked out of the window.

I could feel his gaze. "Are you okay with that?" he said.

"I don't have a choice, do I?"

"No."

"So," I said. "Back to the way things were."

As we approached the airport, he said, "What did you learn?"

He didn't wait for a reply. Instead, he went on: "You learned to sit, you learned to wait, you learned to beg, you learned to bark, you learned to come when you're told to."

He fell silent. Then he said, "What I learned is that you make an enchanting slave."

He unloaded my suitcase, pinched my left nipple, tightened his fist in my hair—and kissed me gently, so gently. Inside, I crumpled up.

"Bye, my little sex kitten."

"Bye, David."

He waved as he drove off. I watched until he was out of sight, then went into the terminal.

SEVEN

SHOULD I tell her?

But how can I put it into words?

The waiter brought two cups of coffee. Sally lit a cigarette. A sparrow hopped onto the next table and pecked at some crumbs.

I decided to try.

"I had a weird experience while I was in California last month," I said.

Sally dragged on her cigarette. "Oh, really? What was that?" she said.

I stirred my coffee. What to say?

Do I say, "I spent two weeks as a sex slave"? No. That sounds ridiculous.

What about, "I had the most amazing sex"? No. That doesn't describe it—just sounds like it was better sex than usual.

Sally looked at me. "Go on. What was the weird experience?"

"Well—" I said, and stopped. I licked the teaspoon and set it on the saucer. "It was a weird sexual experience." As soon as I said it, I wished I hadn't. It sounded pale and wispy. Remote from what had happened.

She laughed. "Weird? How?"

"Well. I don't know what your experience has been—do you find that sex with most guys is more or less the same?" I said.

"Yes," she said, rolling her eyes slightly. "Yes." She laughed. "Some of them like to carry you about more than others. But that's about it."

"This was different. Totally different."

The ash from her cigarette fell onto the table. She didn't notice.

"What do you mean?" she said.

I rubbed my lip. David flashed into my mind. *I am naked, kneeling in front of him, every muscle taut, waiting, not knowing, hardly breathing. He leans toward me—*

"What do you mean?" Sally said again, zapping me back into now.

"I don't know how to describe it. I guess—" I stopped.

Sally was looking at me, her face expectant.

A memory from years before came into my head. I am naked. Bobby is whispering, "I'm going to kiss you all over." He begins kissing my neck, my shoulders, my ears. I know I am supposed to find this sexy, romantic. But while my body is lying there being kissed (now he's at the small of my back, now at the back of my knees), my mind is thinking about calculus problems, and whether anyone might have taken my clothes out of the dryer.

"Go on," said Sally.

Okay. Time for the full confession.

"Well, to be honest, Sally, before this happened, I'd sort of given up on sex. I mean, it was okay, nice to be close to someone and all that. But I'd find my mind wandering off in the middle, thinking about whether to have pizza or pasta for dinner."

I paused. "Actually, it's worse than that," I said. "I sort of felt dead." As I said it, I flushed.

"Sex made you feel dead?"

"Yes. Disconnected. Bored." Does that describe it? Not really. "Absent. As though part of me was asleep," I said. I sipped my coffee.

"But not this time?" she said.

"No." *He is twisting his hand in my hair, forcing my face upward—*

"So what was different?" she said.

Now the hard part. How do I—how can I convey what it was like?

"It was—" I stopped. I decided to use an analogy I'd thought of a few days before. "It was total sex."

"Total sex?" She looked blank.

"Yes. Like total war. You know, war on all fronts. War of annihilation." I paused and looked at her face. Was the analogy working? Not sure. I went on, "Total sex is sex on all fronts. Total engagement of the senses."

She said, laughing, "Ending in annihilation?"

"More or less, yes." *I am just there, listening to the noises of the night.*

"It sounds amazing," she said, stubbing out her cigarette. "How does he do it?"

Since getting back to London, I'd thought of little else.

"He talks," I said. "I've never been with a guy who talked during sex before."

"What does he talk about?" she said. "The stock market? Sweet nothings?"

I felt myself blush. "It's a stream of instruction and invective," I said. "I know it sounds silly, but it's really clever," I said, hurrying on, not wanting to see her amused smile. "It stops the mind from wandering off. And it—" I felt myself blush more than ever. "It takes away self-consciousness and inhibition."

I heard him again. *"Louder! I can't hear you!"*

"PLEASE!" And I am shouting and yelling and forgetting. Forgetting I shouldn't make noise in case someone hears. Forgetting to be restrained. Forgetting the past, the future. Forgetting myself. Just yelling.

She raised her eyebrows. "That's it? That's total sex?"

I swallowed. "No. That's just part of it."

I looked at her. How is she going to take it? I heard him saying, "Be careful when you talk about it. People either get this shit immediately or they look at you like you're nuts."

"It's—" I stopped. "It's an extraordinary mix of brutality and gentleness," I said. *He kisses me gently—so gently that I gasp.*

"Brutality? What do you mean?"

I stalled for time, and called the waiter to ask for two glasses of water.

Eventually I said, "He beat me."

Damn. That doesn't capture the magic of it.

The intimacy. The vulnerability. The trust.

The power.

I discovered I was playing with the coffee spoon, twirling it round and round in my fingers. I glanced up. Sally was staring at me. I couldn't read the expression on her face. I looked at the coffee spoon again.

"You mean, he put you over his knee and spanked you?" she said.

"No." No. *He is kneeling between my thighs. "Hold your ankles, Bitch. I'm going to give ten strokes to the inside of each thigh—"*

"Well what then?" she said.

"He beat me with a riding crop. Or a stick. Or a belt." It sounds so banal.

"Didn't it hurt?" she said, looking horrified.

"Yes. But that's not the point." *I am floating.*

She shuddered. "I don't like pain," she said.

"I don't, either," I said.

"I don't get it. If you don't like pain, why did you let him beat you?" she said.

Let him? I didn't let him. He just did it. *Don't say that. She'll freak.*

"It's odd," I said. "Being beaten—" I paused. *It quiets your mind and opens you to pleasure.* "It turns off the internal monologue."

"Why would you want that?"

I shrugged. "Stops me thinking about pizza or pasta."

She frowned. *She thinks I'm nuts.*

For a moment, neither of us spoke. Then I added. "It's strange. It really does produce annihilation. Afterward, you feel as though you're floating. It's like being in an altered state—you can't do anything, or think about anything."

The sparrow got bolder, and stole a bit of bread from under our table. Sally lit another cigarette. I wished I hadn't started talking.

"Are you sure it's a good idea to let a guy hit you?" she said. "It sounds totally fucked up."

I tossed some crumbs to the sparrow.

"I think it takes a lot of skill to do what he does," I said. *"I'm careful," he whispers.*

"Are you kidding me?" she said. "You think it takes skill to hit someone?"

"Yes." I ignored the hostility in her voice. "I think it must be difficult to know how hard to hit, to know how to read the other person's responses. To generate a feeling of safe danger."

"What do you mean?"

I thought for a moment. "Exploring places you don't normally go, scary places, with someone you trust. It's very controlled."

The waiter came over. "Can I get you ladies anything else?" he said.

"No, thanks, just the bill," said Sally. As the waiter went off, she turned back to me and said, "Who is this guy?"

I smiled. "We met when we were eleven," I said. "My family spent that year in Miami—my dad was posted there for work. David and I went to the same swimming pool. I had a crush on him."

I had a dim memory of a boy with dark curly hair. He was talking to another girl. I stood watching him, wishing he'd pay attention to me.

"At the end of the year, we moved back to Germany. I didn't think I'd ever see him again. But when I came to the U.S. for college, it turned out he'd picked the same one."

"Did he remember you?" she said.

I paused. "I'm not sure," I said. "I guess if we hadn't taken some classes together, we wouldn't have become friends. But we used to study together for exams. And we lived in the same dorm junior year."

"How often do you see each other?"

"A couple of times a year. He moved to the Bay Area after college, and you know I often go out west to work in the archives there. And he sometimes travels to Europe on business—he's one of those consultants, you know, one of those guys who's always on the road. He stayed with me here a couple of times."

"He stayed with you? Had you had sex with him before?"

"No. He never so much as tried to kiss me before. I never thought he was interested in me. He used to flirt aggressively, with lots of innuendo, but before this, that was all it was—flirting."

I saw him standing outside the campus coffee shop. It's summer: he's wearing shorts and a T-shirt, and he has a tennis racquet slung over his back. He's just bought one of those hard, long Italian biscuits with nuts. He dips it into my coffee, covering the end with milk foam, then holds it erect between finger and thumb and offers me a bite. I look at him. He raises an eyebrow. I take the dare. I lower my head toward the biscuit. Two things happen. The biscuit moves down: I have to chase it. And he puts his other hand flat on the back of my neck, and pushes. Gently, but firmly. For an instant. A shiver runs down my back, and my nipples tingle. When I raise my head, we gaze at each other, and he eats the rest of the biscuit, pausing only to offer me the last bite, so that I'd have had to brush his fingertips with my lips. I shake my head. He shrugs, and pops it into his mouth.

I looked at Sally. "I always wanted to go to bed with him, though. Even in college." I laughed. "There's always been something about him. I guess you'd call it animal attraction." I paused. "And, okay, I know this is silly, but I often dream about him," I said.

"The man of your dreams, eh?" she said, her voice sarcastic.

I shrugged. "I always thought he and I would be good together." I realized I sounded wistful.

"Are you going to see him again?"

"No."

"Why not?"

"He's married."

She sat back in her chair and vigorously stubbed out her cigarette. "Married men are scum," she said. "Creeping furtive lying shits. Bored with their wives but too gutless to leave."

"This one wasn't furtive. His wife knew all about it," I said.

Sally raised her eyebrows. "What?"

"Seriously. She knew. I think she thought it was sexy."

I left Sally at a bus stop, and walked back through the park. Had it been a mistake to tell her? Probably. I thought of the appalled look on her face when I'd told her about Maria. The questions she'd asked. *The wife knew? Are you sure he wasn't just saying that? Isn't that a bit creepy?* "It's a little weird, yes," I'd said.

I replayed the conversation in my head, thinking of other things I could have said.

"Creepy? Absolutely. It made me feel like a toy for the two of them." *If you beat her, does she cry? You made my wife happy . . . happy . . . happy.*

Or, "I think she's playing out one of her fantasies." One of my fantasies. *I am spread-eagled . . . my lover is ignoring me . . . another woman . . . I'll be fucking my wife . . .*

Should I have told her of my initial hesitations, of how it was only because Maria knew that I had been able to go along with it? That somehow, her knowing had made it seem okay.

I kicked a bottle top that was lying on the path and watched it skitter into the grass. *Hey. That won't do.* No. I scrabbled in the grass until I found it, carried it to a trash can, and threw it away.

At home that evening, I took out a journal. Many of its pages were already filled with ideas and questions for my time in Italy. I sat with my pen poised above the page. But instead of writing, I found my mind wandering off, wondering about David.

I bet he never goes down on anyone. Too demeaning. Is that right? Maybe he does it as a special treat. *I wonder if he's good at it.* He's good at everything else. *As long as he doesn't look up at me; I hate it when guys do that.*

I guess I'll never know.

I began to dream. *He is pushing my legs apart, he is kissing my thighs . . .*

What a shame we didn't have more time together.

Maybe you can see him again. Maybe he'll be in Europe soon. Maybe—

Stop. It's over.

But it wasn't.

A few days later, the messages and telephone calls began.

"My only regret is that I didn't pierce you," he said the first time he called. "I wanted to pierce your labia, so that every time you spread your legs you'd think of me." He laughed. "I was going to take you to a piercing parlor that day in the City—I know a place where I'd have been able to do the actual piercing—but I changed my mind when you nearly fainted into the pork buns."

Jesus.

So that's what the trip to San Francisco had been about.

"Why piercing? I haven't even got my ears pierced."

"I noticed that. But to alter you physically—that's sexy. A ring through one of your labia, so you'd think of me whenever you spread your legs. Or a dog tag hanging from your tit. A dog tag that on one side says 'David's bitch,' and on the other, my phone number."

That's horrible.

Yet the little hairs on my arms stood on end. A treacherous dampness seeped between my legs.

Does Maria have a dog tag dangling from her nipple?

I pointed out that as he'd intended to abandon me the next day, piercing would have been cruel.

"Sometimes you have to be cruel to be sexy," he said.

Sometimes—what?

I shivered. Somewhere, in a distant corner of my brain, an alarm bell started clanging. But I muffled the clapper in cotton wool, and ignored it.

Later, as I was falling asleep, my mind began to imagine him piercing me. *He is bending between my open thighs. In his right hand he holds a piercing gun. "No, David—" A jolt of pain. He smiles a small smile and strokes my hair. "Good girl. Good girl." And I am wearing a tag that carries his name.*

I almost wished he had done it.

A day or two later, I sat at the kitchen table and wrote him a thank-you letter:

> *Dear David,*
> *As the fortnight in California recedes into the past, it begins to seem more strange, more powerful. I feel like Sleeping Beauty: after years of slumber, I've been fucked awake.*
> *Thank you.*

I added:

> *PS. I've thought of a name for what you do. It's Total Sex.*
> *PPS. I've started to find shoelaces rather erotic!*

He called when the letter arrived. "Did you find it powerful?" he said.

"Very," I said.

But it's over. It has to be.

So when he called one night and whispered that one day soon I would lie in bed with my head on his chest, and tell him this and that, I said:

"David. Back to the way things were."

"Of course," he said.

Parcels began to arrive. First, a novel he'd enjoyed. A week later, I opened a package to find a book on investing. Taped to the front was a note that said, "Read this and you will be less ignorant." Another time, he sent a mug emblazoned with a photo of the Gates of Hell and a note from him that said, "Be led where you would not go." I filled the mug with coffee, and sat and read the investing book.

He called to tell me that, for the first time ever, he'd spaced out in a business meeting.

"We were in this great building in Shanghai. Super view. I looked out of the window and saw those big shipping cranes you like. I thought, 'Kitten likes those cranes.' And suddenly I'm fucking you and I'm smelling you. My hands are on your hips, I hear you begging." He laughed. "I completely lost the thread of the discussion. I've never done that before."

"What happened?"

"I'm pretty good at bullshit." His voice was smug. I wrinkled my nose. *So self-satisfied.*

I pushed the thought away.

———

The next day, Sally called. "Do you want to go to a movie to-night? How about—" and she named a film. "I read some reviews. I think it would interest you."

It was a film about a woman who wants to be beaten, and who finally finds a man who will beat her.

I'd read about it, too. It sounded good.

I hated it. I didn't like watching someone being beaten. I sat hugging myself, bracing my body against the blows of the cane. It wasn't erotic. It was horrible.

And annoying. It didn't capture the essence of what it's like to be beaten. It didn't capture the suspense, or the intimacy. Or what was going on inside their heads. It just looked nasty. If it had been me filming it, I wouldn't have shown how he hit her. I would only have shown their faces.

There was something else I didn't like, as well. Something Sally jumped on immediately.

"She was really fucked up," said Sally, as we sat down in the bar afterward. "All that cutting herself with razor blades, holding hot kettles against her legs to burn herself."

She looked at me, the question unsaid.

"Don't worry. I never did any of that stuff," I said, wishing again that I had never confided in her. "I told you: I don't like pain."

Sally ordered a glass of white wine; I asked for a mojito. I suppressed the urge to spread my legs.

As the waiter went to get the drinks, I thought of myself as a teenager. There I am, screaming at my parents. Now I'm sulking in my room, plotting my own death, imagining how gloomy the funeral will be. I'm out with friends, laughing, watching scary movies, playing pool, discussing how to do fellatio. I'm home, standing in front of a mirror, sucking my tummy in, glaring at my body, wishing my legs were longer, my stomach flatter, my breasts bigger. Now I'm on a diet. But not for long: I'm quickly defeated by a piece of chocolate cake.

"It would never have occurred to me to cut myself," I said. "And I wouldn't have done it if it had. Half the girls in my high school were sticking their fingers down their throats after meals; I couldn't even do that."

I spoke to David about it later. He said, "Yeah, the guys who made that movie didn't get it. It's stupid to think self-harm has anything to do with being a bitch. Being a bitch is about surrender, giving up control. It has nothing to do with liking pain or wanting to be hurt."

Another day, I said, "You know what you said about trust? You know, that you have to trust someone to put yourself in their power?"

"Yes," said David.

"Does it work the other way, too?"

"You mean, do I have to trust a bitch before I can beat her?"

"Yes."

Silence. Then, "Yeah."

"Why?"

"Because in order to beat someone, I have to show myself. The core of myself. It's a very intimate thing to do."

Sally and I had a quarrel. On the telephone. She asked me about my parents. Whether they'd beaten me when I was little.

"What?" I said. "How—" I stopped.

I thought about the birthday parties, the ballet classes, the holidays, about how much they'd sacrificed so I could go to college. I thought about my mother coming to say good night, about my father working late to earn more money. I thought how gentle they both were—to me, to each other—and how shocked they would be by the question, by the thought anyone would ask it.

"No," I said. "They didn't."

Fuck. I threw the phone at the sofa. Maybe it wasn't a good idea to talk about this stuff.

David began to issue invitations.

"I'm going to the Caribbean to go fishing for a few days with some friends. Why don't you come? We'll stay in a great hotel, you can read by the pool while I go fishing, we'll eat together in the evening. I can't wait to watch you sleeping; I bet you look pretty when you sleep."

I saw white sheets, pillows, a balcony with a view of the sea. There I am, in a big hat, meeting David's friends. *And this is my sex slave. How do you do; how do you do.*

"That's not so nice for Maria," I said, frowning.

"These guys are business colleagues. They won't know."

I said no.

"I have a trade show in Vegas at the end of April. Meet me there. We can stay at the Bellagio, see a few shows—"

"I can't: I have to be in London." I hesitated. *Should I say it? No yes.* My pulse began to accelerate. "But I'm giving a lecture in San Francisco at the beginning of May."

SIX

FIRST FRIDAY in May. Ten P.M.

He'll be here soon.

"Can I help with the dishes?" I said, carrying a couple of plates into the kitchen.

"What, when you've just stepped off a plane?" said Kim with a laugh. "No, of course not. We have a machine."

She put down the mugs she was carrying. "We really hope you'll be able to come to the wedding," she said. "We're going to organize a bus trip afterward for the people who've never been to Vietnam before."

"It sounds amazing," I said. "When's it all happening?"

"The wedding's on December 21st," she said. "We're hoping everyone will make a vacation of it, and stay for Christmas and New Year's. I'll send you details in a couple of weeks."

Wind chimes tinkled.

"That's the doorbell," said Paul. "It must be your friend."

It was.

He stood, framed in the doorway, his face in shadow.

My mouth went dry. *Maybe this is a mistake.*

Greetings, introductions, the refusal of a glass of wine. He picked up my suitcase.

"We'll see you at your talk on Monday," said Kim, hugging me.

"Thanks again—and don't forget, I want your cookie recipe," I said. I turned to David. "Can we give Gail a ride home? She's just ten minutes away."

"I'm sorry: my car only has two seats," he said.

Liar.

I stared at him. He winked. In my mind, a voice, just audible, whispered, *selfish bastard.* When we got to the car, he kissed me savagely, roughly, greedily.

"How's my sexy bitch?" he said, twisting his hand in my hair.

Nervous.

"Has she forgotten how to sit?" His voice was hard.

I licked my lips. My legs began to open. Wider, wider. My nipples hardened, poking against the cloth of my bra. I could see from his face that he knew.

"Good girl." He turned the key in the ignition.

We drove past a country club—a waiting list of seven years, and a joining fee of $70,000, David told me; he was on the waiting list—and turned into the hills. I began to imagine what the house might be like. My mind envisioned a four-poster bed standing alone in a room, shackles at the corners. *I am naked, spread-eagled . . .*

We crested a hill and turned into a driveway. "Here we are," said David. He parked, and we got out.

He swept the air with a hand. "I own everything you see," he said.

I looked around. A small lamp was casting a puddle of light at the top of a concrete path. Apart from that, it was dark. I couldn't see anything.

"Impressive," I said, stifling a giggle.

We walked down the path to his house.

The path was steep. Every so often, another puddle of light showed the way, and gave me glimpses of a border, planted along the path. He was talking, "This is a difficult house in the rain . . . Maria wants to plant olive trees, make olive oil . . . we're thinking of getting a dog . . ." but I was only half listening. I was waiting to see the house.

Then, a peaked roof loomed against the sky. I saw a green front door lit from above. A tree in a pot sat next to the door.

At the door, he stopped. Like an egg conjured from nowhere, the leash appeared in his hands. "Are you going to wear the leash as you enter my house?"

No.

We gazed at each other.

My neck bent, my head bowed. He slipped the chain around my neck and, holding the other end of the leash in his hands, pushed open the door and led me inside. I followed. *Like a dog.* No. *Yes.* I swallowed.

I glanced about. We were in a large room with bookcases at one end and a table in the middle.

"I'll show you around later," he said, pulling the leash and leading me down a corridor, past a couple of doorways, and into a bedroom.

A normal queen-sized bed with white sheets stood against a set of windows. A closet with a floor-to-ceiling mirror made up the opposite wall. A white bathrobe hung on a peg by the door.

I caught a glimpse of myself in the mirror. I looked more pale than usual; the metal of the leash, a silvery contrast with my hair. He looked darker. As though we were yin and yang.

But I didn't have long to think about it. He cupped my chin and kissed me languidly, tenderly. I quivered.

"Welcome to my home, Kitten."

He stripped me slowly, taking his time undoing the buttons on my shirt, the hooks on my bra, until I was naked but for the leash.

"On the bed. Your back to the mirror. Show me pretty dog. What do you say?"

He was demanding, but gentle. He did not beat me.

Later, I watched him sleeping. His face had an unfocused expression. It was so different from his usual intensity that he almost looked like someone else. He'd put a pillow between his knees. Funny. I do that.

He began to snore. I slipped out of bed. The floor was rough underfoot, and cold. I tiptoed to the doorway, wrapped myself in the bathrobe, and crept into the passage. Left? Right? I paused, then turned left. The passage shunted me into a small, open room with a fireplace on one side and a sofa staring blankly at a television on the other. Next to the fireplace, a door opened onto a sundeck.

Outside, the wood of the deck was still warm to the touch, or perhaps it was just the contrast with the stone floors of the house. I looked up at the stars. The moon, which had been up when we arrived, had already set. It was dark. Quiet. And far away from neighbors. *No one to hear you scream.* I shivered. As if in sympathy, a sudden gust rustled the leaves on the trees.

I slid back inside, and continued my illicit, self-guided tour. The small room opened into a kitchen that was long and thin like a railway carriage.

Everything is so clean. That must be Maria.

The only other time I'd been to a place David lived in had been—when? Ten years ago? Yes, that's right: he and Maria had just met, and he was living in a tiny apartment in San Francisco.

I saw the two of us arriving there. "Sorry to leave you here, but there's something I've got to take care of. I'll be back in half an hour," he was saying.

"That's fine. See you soon," I said. The door closed behind him, and I was alone. I looked around.

Christ, it was squalid. The kitchen was filthy, stacked with dishes encrusted with food. The bathroom—ugh. The toilet bowl was stained dark brown, and there were sticky drips of urine on the floor; the sink was streaked with old toothpaste. The table in the main room was invisible beneath tumbling piles of papers; atop one there was a wooden African fertility figure, rudely carved, extravagantly endowed. I gaped at it, uncomfortable with its aggressive sexuality. There was nowhere to sit except his bed.

Then, as now, I prowled, full of that mix of curiosity and inhibition that comes from being alone in an apartment that's not yours. I touched nothing, opened no drawers. But the closet door was ajar, so I peeked. Just clothes. No: not just clothes. On a peg, a pair of handcuffs. *Remember how shocked—thrilled—you were?*

He had come back and found me sitting, awkward and blushing, on his bed. He had sat beside me, close, too close. My body had tingled and I had wanted to pull him toward me, to kiss him, to feel his body on mine. No matter that he was a friend. No matter that I was still trying to make things work with Bobby. But he did not touch me, and I did not dare.

Now, part of me wondered, *What if you had got together then? Would it be you living here instead of Maria?*

I shook my head to get rid of the *what if* and discovered I'd walked out of the kitchen and into an enormous cavern of a room. Ah—there's the front door, that's where we came in, and yes, there are the bookcases. So this passage over here on the right—this must be how we got to the bedroom. Yes. I smiled as a small snore rumbled toward me.

I wandered over to the bookcases. Thrillers, modern fiction, nineteenth-century classics. Books on investing; books we had in college. Cookbooks. Battered travel guides. Volumes of poetry, a stack of plays.

One shelf was empty of books. Instead, it had a collection of photographs, in frames. One showed David with his parents and his brother, all wearing silly party hats and laughing. Another was of Maria and a slim, dark-eyed girl. *That must be her daughter.* I looked at the daughter, wondering what she was like. I remembered David saying, "When she was thirteen, she used to practice flirting on me." "That must have been odd," I'd said. "It was," he'd replied.

By now, my feet were cold and I was starting to feel sleepy. I turned away from the bookshelves and set off down the corridor that led to the bedroom.

A door on the left was ajar. I glanced in. Ah. This must be the main bedroom; he and I must be in a guestroom.

I stood in the doorway, hesitating. Inhibition said no. Curiosity said yes. They held a brief tug-of-war. Inhibition tumbled over. I listened. Another snore. And another.

I went in, and switched on the light.

The room was big and strewn with rugs. During the day it must be bright—two of the walls were glass. A big bed sat in the middle. It wasn't a four-poster, either. I felt vaguely disappointed. At the far corner of the room, a door stood open. I walked over and peered around it. I found myself looking into a huge walk-in closet. Racks of dresses, piles of shoes. *She really does have a shoe fetish.* Try some on—what about that pair there, with the straps? *Don't be stupid.* I continued peering. No handcuffs this time—or not that I could see. A couple of scent bottles sat on a shelf. I picked up one and sniffed the nozzle. Light, flowery. Expensive. *So that's what she smells like.* I put the bottle down and listened.

Another snore. I tiptoed to the bed and sat on it, imagining for a moment that this was my bed—our bed. I gave an experimental bounce. The bed creaked. *Silly girl. You'd better not let him find you here.*

Right. I stood up. As I did so, I noticed a small, pale sculpture standing on a shelf by the door. I went over to it and picked it up. Immediately, I wished I hadn't. It was a statue of a naked woman kneeling. But where her head should have been, there was a dog's head. I winced, and put it back where I found it.

"Is my bitch prying?" said a voice.

I jumped, and flushed crimson. *Oh God. He's going to beat you.*

I turned to find David leaning against the doorjamb, his cock erect.

"I'm sorry, I couldn't sleep—"

"It's always nice to see a girl blush to her tits," he said. I looked down. The bathrobe had come open and my breasts were bare. And pink. The realization made me blush more.

"Maria bought it. She's got some others—I'll show you in the morning. But now, since my bitch is awake, it's time she serviced her master again." He reached out and pinched my left nipple. "Bedtime," he said, pulling. He led me by the nipple back to the bedroom. I trotted after him, staring at my nipple in his hand, prickling with humiliation. And desire.

———

He is sleeping again.

I cannot.

The bed is soft, and he is heavy. Unless I lie on the edge, I roll into him.

Can't sleep touching someone. Never have been able to. Need to lie flat.

Tired.

He is warm. Lie against him.

Warm.

Drifting.

Someone is kissing my chin, my earlobes, my temples.

David!

I stretched and opened my eyes.

"Morning, Kitten."

He's on one elbow, looking at me, smiling. A tender, gentle smile. One hand runs up my body, fingers caressing my hip, dancing on my nipple, stroking the back of my neck.

I can feel my face grinning.

"Morning, David."

I snuggled against him.

His knee against my knees, driving them open. Both knees between my knees, splitting my legs apart.

His arms are around me, his weight is on top of me, my legs are open. I am waiting.

"Please," I whisper.

"Please what?" in my ear.

"Please fuck your bitch."

He does.

He handed me the bathrobe. "Put this on. Let's make some breakfast."

The kitchen was full of sunlight.

"Go ahead and make coffee if you want—I don't drink it, but Maria does. All the stuff's on that shelf." He waved at a shelf by the fridge. "How about some juice?"

"That would be great. I can do it."

I opened the fridge and took out a big bottle of orange juice. He handed me two glasses, then started breaking eggs into a bowl. "I thought we'd have omelets today and pancakes tomorrow," he said.

I put the kettle on, and blinked back the sudden tears in my eyes.

It's been ages since someone made breakfast for you.

We took our plates onto the deck and ate looking out at the bushes and the trees.

"I have a present for you," he said.

"What is it?" I said.

"I think you're going to like it," he said.

"What is it? Tell me!"

"Hold on," he said. He went inside and came out with a collar. A beautiful, wide leather collar.

I felt a wild, soaring relief. *At last.*

I knelt on the deck. He looked down at me, and held it out for me to look at. The leather was soft, but not plain; instead, it had three metal rings studded into it, and a wide metal buckle. Gently, he lifted my hair off my neck, and circled it with the collar, fastening the buckle snug, but not too tight, at the back.

He pulled the bathrobe off my shoulders. It slid onto the ground, and I knelt, naked in the sunshine, at his feet.

"You are so beautiful," he said. "Go and look in the mirror."

Dark leather against pale skin. I felt alive, and free.

"Oh, David, thank you," I said, coming back outside. I sat by his feet, and rested my head on his knee. He stroked my hair.

"I thought you'd like it. You've been waiting your whole life for someone to give you one, haven't you, Kitten?"

I nodded.

Silence. A riot of thoughts in my head.

Tell him. He will understand.

I looked up at him. "I bought myself a collar once," I said. "No, twice."

"Did you?" He gazed at me.

"Different places, different men," I said. "But it wasn't any use."

"Tell me," he said.

I swallowed. "The first time, I'd run out to the grocery store to do some last-minute shopping. I was making a dessert and I'd forgotten to buy cream. So I'm in the supermarket, and I'm walking back from the cream section to the checkout with three cartons of heavy cream in my basket. By chance, I walk down the aisle where they shelve pet food and kitty litter, and I suddenly noticed that they had dog collars . . . not fancy collars, but those chains—"

"Chokers? Like the one I put on you the day I took you to the City?"

"Yes. That's right. And on the spur of the moment, I grabbed one, and added it to the basket."

He smirked. "So now you have three bottles of cream and a dog collar in your basket."

"Yes. And I'm in line at the checkout, I'm spacing out, thinking about something else, when the check-out guy says, 'What sort of dog do you have?'"

"I said, 'What?'"

"He said, 'What sort of dog do you have?'"

David started laughing.

"And I'm standing there thinking, dog, what do you mean, dog? They're for me."

"What did you say?" said David.

"I said, 'Whippets.'"

David laughed, twisted his hand into my hair, pulled me toward him, and kissed me roughly.

"I don't know where it came from," I said. "I've never had a dog, let alone a whippet."

"Your subconscious knows who you are, Kitten," he said. "Better than you do. Go on. What happened next?"

"When I got home and produced the collar, I was met with a blank stare. Sam had no idea why I would want one."

I fell silent, remembering the confusion on his face as I'd tried to explain. A wave of sadness crashed over me.

"Kitten? Are you okay?" David sat beside me, and took me in his arms, rocking me, holding my head against his chest. One of his chest hairs tickled my nose.

I nodded, and nuzzled his neck. A scrub jay flew over, and landed on the railing of the veranda. It cocked its head at us for a moment, then flew away. In the distance, a dog barked.

"Want to tell me about the other time?" he said, his voice gentle.

I nodded, and smiled. He shifted a little so he could watch my face.

"I bought my second collar in London, about a year ago. At a shop called Paradiso." I thought of the clean space of the shop, the glass cases with jeweled handcuffs and glittery domino masks. "I saw it in the window as I was walking past. It's beautiful—a plain, wide metal collar, with a ring at the front to attach things to. The only thing is, it's a little tight."

David put his hands around my neck, and squeezed, a little. I shivered, and bit my lip. A small gasp slipped out of my mouth. He smiled.

"I bought matching shackles, too." I paused. "It was while I was apartment hunting, and I was staying with Ian—that guy I met in grad school, the one I really liked."

"That brooding philosophy guy you told me about?"

"Yes."

I saw myself sitting at a kitchen table drinking tomato juice. Ian was opposite me, absorbed in the book he was reading. I watched his hands as they turned the pages and wished I could get up and stroke his neck.

"Go on," said David.

"I thought maybe the collar would get his attention. I knew he likes bondage stuff, he's got tons of bondage porn." I thought of the shelf of videos beneath the shelf of Greek philosophers. "So I slipped into a silk negligée, put on the collar, and the cuffs, and waited for him in his bed."

"And?" said David.

"When he came in, he sat on the bed, and he stroked my hair. He held me. And then he took off the collar, and put it on the pillow."

"That's it? He didn't even fuck you?"

"No."

"Why not?"

I shrugged. "I don't know. We never talked about it."

"You're such a sexy bitch. Buying your own collars." David shook his head and snorted. "Those guys! What were they thinking! You picked badly, Kitten. So many men would have done anything to come home and find you in their beds wearing a collar. I'd have fucked you till you couldn't walk. Then I'd have turned you over and fucked you again. I think I might fuck you again right now."

He picked me up and carried me back to the bedroom.

"Touch yourself."

. . .

"Please."

"Please what?"

"Please."

"Please *what?*"

"Please can I come?"

"Ten. Nine. Eight."

"Seven. Six. Five."

"Four. Three."

On three, I come.

I giggle.

He does not.

He freezes.

I am fucking a statue.

The statue's face moves. Its eyes narrow, its mouth clamps shut, and ecstasy transmutes to anger.

I hear the giggles falter. My hands clutch at the sheets.

The statue comes to life. He pulls out, strides across the room, and comes back with the stick.

"No, David, no."

"Hold your ankles."

"No."

"Bitch, hold your ankles."

"No, David, come on, this is ridiculous." I squirm and try to get under the covers.

I fail.

He grabs my ankles, wrenches them apart, and starts beating the insides of my thighs. His face is contorted, brutal. Mean.

He has never hit me so hard. The pain is ferocious: concentrated and cutting. My legs are jerking as if they are controlled by a demented puppeteer.

I am screaming. Yelling, screaming, howling. Oh Jesus God, it hurts it hurts it hurts.

This is so unfair.

I begin to cry.

I am struggling, but I cannot get away. And wiggling exposes my buttocks. He starts hitting them, too.

Weeping. I have little pools of tears in my ears. My face is slick.

No more blows. Through the blur of tears I see him put the stick down.

The world goes dark: he is sitting on my face.

His buttocks sit in my tears.

As I cry and struggle and gasp for air, he jacks off, until he comes on my breasts.

I hear the door close.

I am alone.

I find a towel to wipe my face, my body. I run my finger along one of the welts on my thighs. The slightest pressure hurts.

I curl up, hugging my knees, and sob into the pillow.

Soon, misery turns to rage. He hit me like that because I came before he said I could? That's ridiculous. Disproportionate. Mean.

Sunlight on the pillow. A voice in my ear.

"Is my bitch going to sulk all afternoon?"

"What did you do that for? It wasn't called for."

He shrugged.

Sunlight in his manner. Jollity.

"Please, leave me alone. Give me some time. I'll be all right."

Alone with the sunlight.

He is back. He climbs onto the bed, spreads my legs, and over my protests, enters me again.

Treacherous body!

I am still angry—so angry. But as he takes what he wants, my body leaps toward him, strong pleasure suffusing my groin.

I moan. I can't help it.

In that instant I began to feel I was keeping company with a powerful magician.

"Touch yourself."

"No." I wasn't making that mistake again.

He takes my hand, places it on my clitoris, and begins to count. This time, it works.

"Now we're back on track," he says, fucking me vigorously, taking his pleasure.

Quiet. For a while we lay together, my legs over his, his arms around me, holding me against his chest. Floating.

"Where's Maria?"

"She's taken her mother away for the Mother's Day weekend." He paused, then said, "She feels vulnerable."

I looked at him in surprise.

He went on, "You're the sort of person I was expected to marry. If you weren't an old friend, she'd join us in a second. Maria slept with women for years. If I said I wanted a threesome just for the hell of it, she'd bring me a girl."

Silence.

Then he said aloud, though so musingly that it seemed he was talking to himself, "You should never sleep with old friends."

Silence.

I began to feel wakeful. I propped myself on one elbow, and started to explore his body. It was the first time I'd had the chance: it was the first lazy time we had had together.

He had scars just above the armpits, at the place where the arms join the shoulders at the front. I ran my fingers down them, shallow gullies on a relief map.

"What are these from?" I asked, thinking he might have had surgery.

"Stretch marks from weight lifting," he said.

I traced the line of his neck, down to the little hollow at the base of his neck where the clavicles come together. Here, his skin was soft. I caressed it: it's such a vulnerable place.

I ran my hands down his back. The skin was smooth and soft, so soft it almost felt like it wasn't there. I stroked him, wanting to remember the sensation.

His thighs were strong, heavy. His feet were elegant, his toes straight.

"This is my favorite part of your body," he said, putting his hand onto my hip. "It fits into my hand so perfectly when I pull you to me as I'm taking you from behind."

———

"Maria left a couple of skirts for you," he said, pointing.

What?

I looked over. Two black skirts lay on top of a chair.

"Why?"

"I told her you didn't have any. She picked out a couple she thought you'd look good in."

Who is this woman? How can she—?

I flushed.

"That's how I know she's the right woman for me," he said, with a big smile.

I had already known that he and I—that it was just a fling, that he was just playing around. I didn't matter. I knew that.

I knew that this man who made me feel so—what? Cherished, cared for, adored—was never going to be someone I could be with.

I looked down. I didn't want him to see the wistfulness on my face.

Someone's going to get hurt, and it's probably going to be you. No. *Yes.*

"Try them on," he said. "When you're dressed, I'll take you to dinner."

They both fitted.

I chose the more flattering one and put on a shirt I had that happened to go quite well.

A small blond woman in high heels, a just-above-the-knee-length skirt that had a slit running up the left thigh, and a décolleté black shirt gazed at me from the mirror.

I ran a comb through my hair.

"Ready."

He laughed. "You take less time to get ready than any woman

I've ever met." He looked at me. "That's screamingly sexy. You wearing my wife's skirt."

"You like it that I'm wearing Maria's clothes?"

"I like what it says about her."

What it says about her. I bit my lip and stared at the ground.

"I've picked this great new Japanese place," he said, as we walked to the car.

A waiter led us to a table. As we sat down, David said, "You're glowing. Everyone is staring at you."

They'd be staring even more if they knew I was wearing Maria's skirt.

I thought of what Sally would say if I told her. "You wore his wife's skirt? To a restaurant? Are you insane?"

For a moment I imagined telling her about the afternoon. "He punished me for reaching orgasm too early—beat me really badly, I've never screamed so much. Afterward I was furious; I thought it was totally unfair. But you know the weird thing? When he came back and fucked me again, my body responded to him in a way that it's never responded to anyone. It sort of surged toward him and dissolved in pleasure."

He knew it would. He knows what lurks in the darkest shadows of your psyche. Better than you do.

I bit my lip.

David was talking, telling a story about how, when he was a kid, his father had always come to watch his tennis games. "At the time, I didn't realize how difficult it must have been for him to do it—he was working at this super-high-stress law firm—but somehow, he always managed to get away so he could be there for me."

The food came; the conversation shifted.

"Tell me about the statue," I said.

"What, the one in the bedroom?"

"Yes," I said.

"Do you like it?" he said, feeding me a piece of sushi.

No.

"I'm not sure," I said.

He smiled. "Maria found it in a gallery in San Francisco. We'd been thinking about the perfect pet. She thought this symbolized everything I was looking for. The obedience and loyalty of a dog; a body you can fuck. The ultimate bitch."

The ultimate bitch.

I shivered.

"Let's go," he said. "I want to fuck you again."

By the end of the weekend, his penis was chafed raw. I could barely walk. Just as a sailor freshly onshore feels the earth moving, my body felt as though it was fucking even when it wasn't, and my head echoed with commands, like a song you can't stop humming. *Beg, offer yourself, please, ten nine, offer yourself, sit, eight seven, please, no, please, six five, lick my asshole, drink, four three, can't hear you, two one, louder, come. . . . Beg, ten nine . . .*

"I thought about how I could improve on total sex," he said. "I decided on total sex all the time."

He did laundry. Towels and sheets. He made the bed, fluffing the duvet, plumping the pillows and cushions. He looked at them, pleased. Perfect.

I watched as he erased my presence from the house.

"What do you want for dinner? Spaghetti?" he said, his voice warm.

He wasn't talking to me. He was sitting on the steps of the deck, on the telephone to Maria, again.

If only I could have spirited myself away.

I walked over to the far corner of the deck and leant against the railing. I looked out at the yard, and tried to close my ears.

"Let's go." That was for me.

"Are we stopping for lunch?"

"No. I haven't got time. I'll drop you at your hotel." He picked up my suitcase, and led the way to the car.

I swallowed. I felt hollow and flat. And hungry.

And alone.

I sat in bed at the hotel, drinking a glass of red wine. I glanced at the clock. Two A.M. I smiled.

What a success!

I wasn't thinking about the lecture, though I'd been nervous and it had gone well. I was thinking about how I'd worn one of his leather shackles strapped around an ankle as part of my outfit. *It looked like part of your shoe.* Unless you noticed that it was only on one leg. *Or you knew what you were looking at. The little chain was a giveaway.*

David had known what he was looking at. As he drove me back to the hotel, he said, "You're such a sexy bitch. When I saw you wearing that strap, I wanted to take you with such violence you have no idea." Then he laughed and said, "Well, maybe you have some idea."

"When did you notice?" I said.

"About halfway through."

He came with me to the room.

"Get on your knees. Don't take off your dress. I'm going to beat you, but you can't make any noise. Bite the pillow."

. . .

He put down the stick.

"Beg to have your pussy eaten."

I felt myself smiling.

"Please," I said.

"Please what?"

"Please eat my pussy."

He did.

But oh no! He wasn't good at it. He kept blowing at me, and changing what he was doing. His tongue was too pointy; it sort of hurt.

I'm not going to come.

He seemed to know that, too, because he didn't go on and on. He put my hand where his mouth had been.

"Touch yourself."

. . .

"Ten . . ."

Later, lying with my head on his chest and his arms around me, I said, "David?"

"Yes, Kitten?"

"When you go down on me—it might work better if you kept your tongue flatter."

He lifted me off his chest and rolled over to look at me.

His face was dark.

"Is my bitch telling me how to eat pussy?" he said.

He's angry. He's going to beat me again.

No. He's not.

He smiled and said, "You can always tell me what you like, Kitten. I won't always give it to you—but you can always tell me."

All the tension left my shoulders and I found myself curling against him, kissing his neck, his ears, running my hands through his hair. "Thank you," I whispered.

Lying together. In silence.

Then he spoke. "Who's crazy about his bitch?" he said.

I propped myself on my elbow and looked at him.

He had his eyes half closed.

"Are you, David? Are you?"

He nodded.

"Crazy, crazy."

I found I was smiling a gigantic smile. I put my arms around him and pulled him to me, hoping he wouldn't notice the tears in my eyes.

Later. "I've got to get home. Don't move."

He gazed at me from the doorway. I could see him study the muss of my hair, the flush of my cheeks, the fling of my arms on the bed, the riding crop on the pillow. He seemed to memorize each wrinkle of the dress crushed up around my waist. He lingered over the splay of my legs with their mix of bruises and fresh welts; his eyes dwelt on my feet still in their high heeled sandals, on the strap buckled around my ankle.

He stood in silence, looking.

"Bye, Kitten," he said. The door opened, shut, and he was gone.

FIVE

TWO MONTHS later, he came to Italy to stay with me for a week.

My apartment was big, with bare wooden floors and huge windows. It felt even bigger than it was because I had almost no furniture.

The sun shone. The summer was hot. The sort of heat that invented the siesta.

In the days before he arrived, I filled my journal with hopes. I was sure that, at last, I was going to reach orgasm during sex without having to touch myself. Without having to pretend I was with someone other than my lover. Without going away in my head.

It was going to happen. By itself. Like magic.

But I was also afraid. *If he can't do it, no one can.*

There were deeper fears, too. I was afraid of him, of where else he might take me, what else he might do. *I don't know what his limits are.* I took out one of the letters he had sent and read it again.

Bitch:
You are naked on your knees, blindfolded. Crimson welts tell of today's thrashings. Purple and green bruises of previous beatings.

"Offer yourself," I say, as I enter the room. And you reach back pulling your cheeks apart, exposing your cunt.

"Please don't hurt me," you say. I snap a pair of alligator clamps onto your labia. One on each side, connected by a silver chain. I slowly tighten the clamps, past throb, past pinch, to bite.

You don't fight, or squirm. You crumple. I give the chain a tug. The jolt causes a stream of whimpers and tears.

"Please, please take them off," you beg.

I walk across the room, select the riding crop, and deliver five vicious strokes to your ass. Each blow makes the clamps bite deeper, sending shocks of pain through your body.

I whisper, "What do you say when your master abuses your cunt?"

I shuddered. Does he really use clamps?

Does he really want to hurt me that much, in that way? I looked at my legs, the pale skin unmarred by bruises and welts, and wondered, did I want them covered in bruises again?

For that matter, did I want to be called "Bitch" the whole time? I read the letter again. *Does he mean it?* I don't know.

But when I wasn't fretting, I was indulging in fantasies of how we'd lie around in the afternoons, reading books together. Perhaps he'd read aloud to me. Maybe we could discuss our favorite poems. And then we'd cook together in the evenings, or perhaps go for a stroll and drink a glass of wine in a bar nearby.

I marked the calendar. *He'll be here in three days.*

A flash of annoyance. *Why do I have to get my period now?*
Settle down. Concentrate. You have work to do.

But instead of sitting at my desk and learning Italian verbs or
reworking my lecture into an article for a magazine, I roamed the
alleys of the old town. I walked past the shop where the mannequins were dressed in flagrantly sexy clothes (*Go in—buy something. Don't be silly. I can't wear that stuff*), down to the flower
stand (a bouquet of irises, please), and on to the bakery where
shelves were piled high with pastries and cakes. As I was passing
a pharmacy, I remembered he'd told me to buy a hand mirror, so
I popped in to see if they had one. They did; I bought it. *Why
does he want you to get a mirror?* I don't know.

At home, I put the irises into a vase, then paced the rooms.
Looks bare. Wish I had more furniture.

Concentrate.

I sat at the desk, then got up again. I glared at the piles of books
and papers. *Wish I had some shelves—this room is such a mess. It's
your study; he won't come in here. But the bedroom.* The bedroom
is fine—you have a big bed, what more do you need? I wandered
in, opened the shutters, and stood gazing out at the piazza with its
fountains and cafés. But then the phone rang and I went into the
sitting room. Once I'd hung up, I looked around at the table, the
pair of chairs I'd bought from the café downstairs, the phone sitting on a cardboard box, the stereo on the floor, and, against the
wall, a single bed I'd borrowed and which I used as a sofa. *It's okay.*
It's empty. *Nonsense. It's the interior-design version of those restaurants where they have huge plates and tiny helpings. Tell him it's
fashionable. But hide that cardboard box.*

I covered the cardboard box with a sarong. Then I noticed that
the light on the phone was flashing.

He'd left a message. "Are you ready for me, Bitch? You better

get lots of sleep before I arrive. By the time I'm through, you're
going to be too tired to chew."

At the airport, waiting. *There he is!*

"David!"

His hands running up and down my body, squeezing my buttocks. *We're in the airport.* His mouth on mine.

"Hello, Bitch."

"The car's over here. David—" *You'd better tell him.* "I've got
good news and bad news."

"Let me guess. You're bleeding."

"Yes . . ."

He shrugged. "So?"

Oh. Right.

"I've booked a restaurant you'll like for dinner tonight," I said,
smiling at him.

But the restaurant was a mistake. After traveling for eighteen
hours, a long lavish meal was the last thing he wanted.

My next mistake was about food. He couldn't read the
menu—so I had to order for him!

Except I ordered food he didn't like. I didn't know that *fegato*
was liver. I thought it was a cut of beef.

We sat outside in a walled courtyard. The stones radiated
heat; he radiated calm tolerance and fed me chocolate ice cream
from a tiny spoon.

He punished me when we got home.

There was a wildness in him that night. The careful control he
normally hit me with was gone. Blows fell without restraint, without number; he hit with the riding crop, the stick, the flat of his
hands; he hit my arms, my legs, my breasts, whatever he could

reach. He hit hard. I howled and screamed. He put his cock into my mouth, but instead of letting me pleasure him, he took my head in both hands and held it while he rammed himself deep into my throat, over and over again.

"Now you know what it's like to have your face fucked, Bitch," he whispered.

I choked and gagged. He turned me over.

"My bitch has forgotten her manners. What do you say?"

"Stop, David, stop. Please stop."

"No, that's wrong. Bitch, what do you say?"

"Please."

"Please what?"

"Please fuck your bitch."

"What are you?"

"Your bitch."

"You're three holes for my cock. Say it."

"No."

"Say it."

I said it.

"How many have I used tonight?"

"Two."

"Beg me to use the third."

"No, please, no, David, please."

"Oh, Bitch, big mistake."

He didn't try to be gentle. He rammed himself into my asshole, pushing in up to his balls in one thrust.

I screamed and screamed and screamed; tears poured down my cheeks. He hit me with the stick; my arms gave way and I fell onto my face. He kept hitting me. He wasn't thrusting, he didn't need to—I was impaled: his dick was getting pleasure from my writhings, and contortions, and attempts to get away. Then he grabbed my hips and fucked my asshole, shaking me as though I were a rag doll.

He kissed me, small kisses on my neck, tender kisses on my nipples, a nibble on my ear.

"What do you say?"

I was too busy sobbing to say anything.

"You say, thank you for using your bitch."

Then, with one arm around me, he slept.

I shivered and whimpered all night.

He was gentle in the morning. But I was angry.

"Why? Why did you have to hit me like that? Why?"

His voice was quiet, hard. "You have no idea how lucky you are. Most bitches would give anything to have an evening like the one I gave you. I used you completely, for my pleasure."

He moved to caress me. I recoiled.

"No. Don't touch me."

He shrugged. And watched me.

After a while, I reached for his hand, opened it, and kissed his palm. I didn't know why.

He put his arms around me.

"Good girl," he whispered. "Good girl."

He stroked my hair, ran his hands over my breasts as though they were the most precious, delicate things in the world. He kissed my eyes. I quivered, and gasped, and found myself relaxing against his chest.

I heard my voice saying, "Please. Please fuck your bitch."

He did. Plain old missionary position—but it was anything but plain now.

I was spellbound, scarcely breathing, transfixed by his face.

Later, we drove to watch the sun set over a nearby lake. People were swimming in the water, or fishing; small boys were skipping stones across the water. Yet it seemed that there was no one there but the two of us, a woman sitting on a wall, a man standing behind her, cupping her breasts, nuzzling her neck, and gazing at the ripples on the water below, at the swifts darting in the sky above as they chased insects in the evening air.

I was still in shock.

"Why so rough, David?"

"Kitten, it will always be like that at the beginning."

What did he mean, always? How long did he think this could go on?

I think that was the moment I began to hope. Stupid, stupid hope.

We watched the swifts wheeling in the sky. The light was soft.

"When my bitch is away from me, she gets uppity—she forgets her manners. She forgets what she is. I have to remind her," he said. He stroked my hair.

"But you've crossed the Rubicon, Kitten. It doesn't get much rougher than that."

I hoped he was right. I ignored the voice that said, *But the Rubicon lies to the south. It's between here and Rome. . . .*

Every day, he called Maria several times.

At first, I skulked in my study, pretending to work, but in fact scribbling over and over again on a piece of scrap paper, *Be strong, be strong, be strong; ignore it, ignore it, ignore it, ignore it; pretend you don't care, pretend, pretend . . . oh please, pretend.*

But then, I overheard him saying, "You think I should shave her pussy? . . . Black jack?" He laughed. "That's a great idea . . ."

No, please, no.

For some reason, I'd thought they'd stopped talking about me. That what he and I did was private. I hadn't realized that Maria— that she was an architect of our time together. That, in some way, she was in the bed with us. That she got to plan how he would humiliate me.

Be strong, be strong, pretend you don't care, pretend, pretend . . .

That's when I started going for a run when he talked to her— better to be out of the apartment, hide from it, not see it.

Once, she called. Her timing was perfect. Moments before, he'd shouted, "Drink, Bitch, drink," and come in my mouth. I was lying between his thighs, my head on his leg, breathing in the musk from his groin. The phone rang; he answered; he kicked me away, left foot to right shoulder. "Did you find it?" he said to the telephone, his voice warm and loving.

My heart flinched. But I smiled at him and kissed his foot— and went running, pounding through the alleys and narrow streets, jumping to avoid the cars and the dog shit, running, sweating, gasping. Fleeing reality.

When I got back, she was gone. He was mine again. For now.

In the late afternoon we went for a walk. "I really like your apartment, Kitten," he said. "It's big and airy and light. I was worried it might be tiny, like that place you had in London."

"I liked that place," I said. "It was cute. I felt good there."

"Yes, but if you stretched, you stubbed your toe on one of the walls," he said.

We passed a shop that was selling ice cream. A crowd stood in front: everyone was eating ice cream. Small children, young men on motorbikes, old men, nuns. Even the pigeons—they were eating the bits of cone that someone had dropped. "We'd better join in," I said. "What flavor do you want?"

Ice creams in hand, we walked on. "This might not be the moment to ask," he said, "but have you been fucking other guys?"

I wanted to laugh. Other guys—there were no other guys.

"How can I?" I said, glancing at him.

He nodded. "Want to do the right thing by Maria. Don't want to go home with herpes."

I looked at the ground, watching the shapes of the paving stones. *That one's a rhombus. That one's a square. Pretend you don't care. Rhombus, rectangle, rhombus.*

"Hey, Kitten, let's go in here," he said, opening the door to a shop full of beautiful fabrics: tablecloths, cushion covers, linens. "I told Maria we'd get her a present."

She wants a present from me? Does she really find this sexy?

I played interpreter as David had tablecloth after tablecloth unfolded and displayed. Eventually he chose one with rich sunset colors. "We're planning a redecoration—I think this'll look good in our new dining room."

"It's gorgeous," I said, trying to sound enthusiastic. Trying to sound as though I enjoyed hearing about their plans for the future. I guess it worked, because the next thing he said was, "Oh, and did I tell you? We're getting a puppy! At the beginning of August. It'll be a bitch, of course." I looked away. *Redecorating his house. A puppy.* I bit my lip. *His life is settled. You are a holiday for him.*

When we got back, he cooked. What a treat! Except: the recipe was from Maria's grandmother. *Maria. Always Maria.*

I was cutting bread when he said—I no longer remember what prompted it—"I think I'm a good husband."

I thought so, too. I saw how much trouble he took to reduce the possible impact that his being here might have on Maria, and I ached to be the focus of so much care. *She must feel so loved.*

He's been here three days. You've had a lot of sex. But you still haven't come without using your hands. There must be something wrong with you. You must be broken. No. Yes.

The contrast between us was unbearable. He was inexhaustible, coming five, six, seven times a day, sometimes beating me, sometimes not, sometimes letting me touch myself and counting for me (Ten, nine . . . three, two, one. Come, Bitch, come now!), sometimes pushing my hands away and just pleasuring himself with my body. It wasn't fair. And he slept while I lay awake. That wasn't fair, either.

Late at night on the third night, exhausted and dazed from another beating, I got up from beside his sleeping body and went and sat naked in my huge empty sitting room, put on some music (quietly, quietly), and wept.

Suddenly, he was in front of me, kneeling, holding me.

"Hey, Kitten, what's the matter?"

"I think I'm broken," I heard myself saying.

"You're not broken, Kitten, there's nothing the matter with you."

"My head gets in the way. I can't come."

"Kitten, Maria had been married for ten years before I met her, and she didn't have her first orgasm during sex until she met me and I fucked her properly."

"But—"

"Kitten, come back to bed. Stop worrying about it." He shook his head. "Sitting here listening to sad music. Silly Kitten."

"But—"

He picked me up and took me back to bed.

"But—"

"Kitten, I know this stuff is hard for you—I knew it the first time I fucked you."

"How?"

"Because I fucked you like a bitch and you didn't come. But you've got it all wrong. Your only problem is that you're one of the most goal-oriented people I've ever met. Stop thinking about the goal. Enjoy the hike."

Then he added, as a sleepy afterthought, "When guys smoke heroin, it's called 'chasing the dragon.' Enjoy the chase, Kitten."

"Yes, but I don't want to chase dragons, I want to catch them."

"You can't go after them aggressively, Kitten. You have to sneak up on them. Stop scaring them away. Now go to sleep. I'm going to fuck you again in the morning and I want you rested."

He held me, and I slept.

Hiking: that was a good way of putting it. Though for me it was all uncharted territory, I felt he was taking me on his favorite hikes, along trails he'd found years ago, to vistas he knew he liked. One morning, he got out the collar he'd bought me, and fastened it around my neck.

"This has some bells and whistles we didn't use last time," he said.

What? Ah. A metal ring on the front.

He turned me onto my back, shackled my ankles to my wrists, and clipped the leash onto the collar. He fastened the leash to the door. And then, while I lay splayed open and helpless, he propped himself up on the pillows, opened a book, and started to read.

And read.

It was strangely upsetting.

After about ten minutes, I heard myself beginning to beg.

"Please. Please, David, please fuck your bitch."

He glanced up, shook his head, went back to his book.

"Please."

"No."

"Please."

Silence.

"Please." I heard desperation in my voice.

He turned another page.

"Please, David, please." I wanted anything—a cock, a dildo, a thumb, anything.

"Shut up, Bitch, I'm reading. If you make one more sound, I'll have to gag you. Is that what you want? One of my socks in your mouth? Is it?"

Then, he leant over—not touching, though my back arched and my body rose up to meet him—and whispered, "It's okay to cry."

I hadn't known I wanted to cry. But suddenly, my cheeks were wet.

"Good girl. It's hard being a bitch and wanting to be used."

I heard myself whimpering, imploring, "Please."

He put the book down, took my hips in his hands, and *wham.*

"Thank you," I whispered.

He left me there, trussed up, semen splattered on my belly, while he ate lunch.

One afternoon, he walked over to me, reached into my shorts, and plunged his thumb into my pussy.

I thought it was a gratuitous act of possession, an unnecessary reminder that he would touch me when he wanted to, where he wanted to, whether I wanted him to or not. But about five minutes later, he walked over, put his fist in my hair so I couldn't escape, and dipped his fingers into my pussy. He licked them, slowly, languidly, luxuriously, as he had licked the ice cream. I shivered with pleasure to see his pleasure in my body. I wasn't ready for what he said next.

"Caramel."

"What?"

"I put a caramel into your pussy. Now you taste of caramel."

So I did. Caramel was melting out of my pussy. My thighs were starting to be wet and sticky with it.

He smiled, went to the closet and picked out a dress. "Put this on. We're going out."

"No, David."

"Yes, Kitten. And no underwear."

How did he make me do it? It wasn't the threat of punishment if I didn't, or the fear of disappointing him. It was the silent force of his eyes that compelled me to strip off my shirt and shorts, take the dress from his outstretched hand, and slip it over my head. He helped me with the zipper.

Ten minutes later, I was sitting outside at a café in the piazza. My dress was sticking to my legs, my legs were sticking to my legs, rivulets of caramel were working their way to my knees. And I was drinking lemonade, and talking, and pretending nothing unusual was going on.

The whole time, he watched me, his eyes leaving my face only to check that my legs were still spread (they weren't—then, as he raised an eyebrow, I found that they were).

Some pretty teenage girls walked past, laughing and chattering. They were slim, and dressed with a simple elegance. "People are stylish here," he said, swiveling his head to look at them as they walked across the square. For a moment, his face became hard, savage, cruel. Or was I imagining it?

Arm in arm, we walked through town. No. That's not right. Arm through my arm, he paraded me through town. My dress was plastered to my legs as though I'd entered a wet T-shirt competition from the crotch down. It was hard to walk. I could feel myself flushing with shame. I was aware of every glance, every noise; I was aware of my body, sweating, blushing, melting; I was, simply, totally, aware.

At last. Home. He stripped off the dress, carried me to the bed, and slowly, slowly, licked caramel from my thighs and groin until I shuddered and moaned and begged to be allowed to come.

He's improved.

"Let's get you cleaned up," he said. "You've got a big night tonight."

Uh-oh.

He carried me to the bathtub and hosed me down, washing my flanks as you might wash a horse after riding. He twisted his hand in my pubic hairs, and tugged.

"I'm going to shave these off."

"No, David."

"Yes. And I'm going to put a dildo inside you while I do it. That's Maria's idea."

I know.

"And then—" But he didn't finish the sentence.

Then—what? I wasn't sure I wanted to find out.

"I'd better go and get some groceries," I said. "We haven't got anything for supper."

"Nice try, Kitten. You're not going anywhere."

He toweled me down, and carried me back to the bed. I started to get up.

"Down, Bitch. Bad dog."

I lay back down. I was starting to be afraid.

"Don't move. Don't even think about it."

He disappeared for a few minutes, and came back with a bowl of hot water, a can of shaving foam, a pack of razor blades, a towel, and a razor. He went to his suitcase and brought out a dildo. Black jack. Oh shit.

"Great dildos, these," he said. "You can put them in the dishwasher. I got it at Stormy Leather. Same place I bought your collar."

He pinched my left nipple, hard. I gasped.

"You bought a hand mirror, like I told you to, right?"

"Yes," I said.

"Where is it?"

"In the bathroom cupboard."

He went to get it. But he didn't give it to me. He put it down beside the razor. I watched with nervous attention.

Black jack—here it comes. Shove. Thanks, Maria.

"Hold it in your pussy, Bitch. Don't let it slide out."

He leant close to me. "You're lucky I don't put it in your asshole." Then he added, "If I had two more, I'd put one in your asshole and one in your mouth. Just to remind you what you are."

I shivered.

He started shaving me. It took an inordinately long time. Black jack slid out. I said nothing. He didn't notice. *Fuck you, Maria.*

"You have a birthmark here," he said, pointing.

I do?

Several razor blades later he said, "That's good enough for government work."

He dried me off, and moved the bowl of foamy, hairy water onto the floor.

"Now we're ready to play."

He picked up the stick, and from his suitcase produced a pair of adjustable alligator clips, joined by a chain.

"No!" I started to get up.

"Yes."

He pushed me down, and fastened the clamps to the lips of my pussy.

I started to scream. And scream. And scream. And scream.

He hit my inner thighs with the stick. Contrasting pain. It's different. The texture is different. Stick is transient; pain crashes and recedes. Each crash distracts from the fierce constant biting of the clamps. But Jesus God, it all hurts. IT HURTS.

I can't scream more than I am screaming already.

"TAKE THEM OFF! DAVID, TAKE THEM OFF!"

"Breathe," he said.

His face was close to mine. "Come on, deep breaths. One, two, three."

I struggled to breathe.

"That's a girl."

I get a little calmer. He holds up the mirror. I can see my pussy. It looks as though it has electrodes fastened to it. I can feel that my eyes are wide, wide open.

He tightens the clamps.

I am screaming again, deep, throaty, howling, panicking screams.

He is fucking me—HE IS FUCKING ME. I am screaming and he is fucking me. He is looking down at my face, he can feel the clamps against his balls, he is fucking me, torturing me, I am screaming.

He stops. He undoes the clamps. Undoing them hurts even more—it's not possible, but it hurts even more. And then it stops.

I am sobbing. Limp and sobbing. I am curled into a fetal position, sobbing.

He turns me over, opens my legs, and fucks me, gently, until he comes.

I am still crying. He is holding me, stroking me, kissing me. He blots away the tears.

"You are so beautiful in pain," he said. "I've never seen anything like it."

I was too obliterated to answer.

The next day, something amazing happened. I caught a dragon.

It was in the afternoon. We'd been fucking all morning. We'd bought lunch from the local bakery, and shared a piece of my favorite dessert, a thick, sticky almond tart topped with caramelized pears. ("Tomorrow we're not sharing," he said, his voice muffled and greedy as he licked his fingers. "I want my own piece.") We'd napped. I'd gone running. We were fucking in the living room. In the sunshine.

"What do you say?"

"Please fuck your bitch."

"Play with the balls. . . . What are you?"

"Your bitch."

When, without warning, without counting, he yelled,

"Come, Bitch, come now!"

Pleasure rippled through me, down to my toes. My back cracked. I gasped, and let out a small moan.

He cuddled me, and smiled, while I wept small tears of huge happiness into his neck.

FOUR

THAT WAS the week he started to smile—really smile. A big, open, relaxed, happy smile. He smiled it more and more as the week went on.

That week, I learned small details about him. My idea of breakfast—coffee with sweet croissants, fresh from the local bakery—was not his thing. He had to eat eggs or meat in the morning, otherwise he felt lousy. He hid it well: the onset of lousiness was marked by a stern, controlled quiet, rather than grouching irritation. But one morning, as we were on our way north to go hiking in one of my favorite spots in the hills, he made it clear that we had to stop to eat emergency meat. I pulled over in the next village we came to, and we sat in the shade in a square by an ancient church, feasting on steak at eleven o'clock in the morning.

As we drove on, he said, "It looks like California."

"Dry with scrubby little oak trees? Yes. Though I always think it looks like a place where giants go bowling, and then don't tidy up—look at these huge rocks scattered everywhere."

We came round a corner and there, before us, was one of my favorite views. Big hills all around, and down in the valley, at the corner, a village with a medieval castle, looking like something from a children's storybook.

"Wow," he said. "Nothing like that in California."

We drove down the steep winding road, then through the narrow streets, parked behind a tiny, ancient church, and started hiking up the hillside. I ran ahead, wanting him to run after me and catch me. But he wouldn't play.

"Come on, David, run after me, try and catch me. Please."

"No, Kitten."

"Please! I love being chased!"

He shook his head and said, "Kitten, one of the things they tell you when you train a dog is that you've got to keep control of the game."

"Meanie."

He shrugged.

I pouted and pretended to be a puppy, running ahead, and back, ahead, and back.

"When I was a little kid, we used to play a game in the school playground called 'kiss, cuddle, or torture,'" I said. "The girls would run away and the boys would run after them, and when you were caught, you had a choice—kiss, cuddle, or torture."

He raised an eyebrow. "And you—"

"I always said 'cuddle.' I didn't want their sloppy kisses. And 'torture' was stupid—having your skirt lifted so the boy could see your underwear."

He laughed. "You were just prudish."

"Shy," I said.

Farther on, he grabbed me. And up there, in the hills, looking down at the village with its vineyards and its castle, he held my arms behind my back, bent me forward, pulled down my shorts, and standing, fucked me hard, savagely, ignoring my struggles, not caring if someone might happen by.

Another detail: he hated shaving because, "You can't win. You do it, then you have to do it again the next day." Emancipated from going to the office, he did not shave every day; his face fast grew rough against my neck, the hairs a prickly contrast to the soft, curly hairs on his head, the long dark hairs on his chest, the luxuriant curls of his groin. It made him look rough and wild and dangerous—a ruffian. I teased him: "Gentlemen prefer blondes but blondes prefer ruffians."

"Ruffian. You like it because it has 'ruff' in it," he said with a bark that made me giggle.

"No, I like it because it has 'rough' in it," I said, falling on him, trying to tickle him.

After a few days, he let me shave him, sitting patiently—for I was cautious and slow. He made me laugh by pulling the faces that men pull so the cheek goes taut enough for the razor. Sitting on his lap, I cut his fingernails. I liked it—I didn't know why.

He did. "It's because you want to serve," he said.

When I went to pee, he pulled open the bathroom door.

"Come on, David. Go away."

"No. I want to watch you piss."

"No, stop it, that's really twisted. Leave me alone."

"Kitten, I want you to forget I'm here. I want you to lose your self-consciousness in front of me. Now, go ahead. Piss."

Silence. He folded his arms and leant against the door. "I'll wait," he said. "We've got all day. Just forget I'm here."

Finally.

"Good girl," he said.

"Pillow fight!" I leapt at him, swinging the pillow with both hands. *Thwack, bam.* Two good hits! I laughed at his look of surprise.

Uh-oh. He's coming for me now.

"That's not fair, you're cheating!" I yelled as he grabbed me around the middle, threw me onto the bed, and tumbled on top of me. He held my wrists in one hand and disarmed me, tossing the pillow to one side.

"Naughty Kitten," he whispered, planting little kisses on my neck, along my ears, under my chin. I murmured and stretched and ran my fingers through his hair. He rocked me, and whispered in my ear, "You know, you whimper when you sleep, Kitten. It's as though you're having bad dreams."

He picked up his camera. "Strip off. I'm going to take a picture of your tits and send it to—" and he named a magazine. "They hold competitions. Guys write in and rate all the photos; I think you'll do really well."

"No, David." My mind recoiled from the idea of strange men looking at my breasts, comparing them with those of other women.

"Go on," he said, gesturing.

"No."

He hesitated. "Are you sure?"

"Yes. It's too public."

He shrugged and put the camera down.

"I don't like the clamps, David."

"Of course you don't, Kitten."

"Why? Why did you use them?"

He said softly, "When I looked down at your terrified face and saw the pain and fear in your eyes, and felt the clamps against my balls as I used the hole I was torturing, I was riding ecstasy."

Jesus.

"I beat you to distract you from the clamps. And I had you breathe deeply to calm you down so I could tighten the clamps, and watch the fear and pain start again," he said.

What sort of monster was I dealing with?

"It's too much," I said. "No more clamps."

He looked at me, his dark eyes fixed on my face.

"Do you think it's a coincidence that when I was fucking you the next day, you came without using your hands for the first time ever?" he said, his voice quiet.

Oh God. Is that what it takes?

"I know what I'm doing, Kitten."

Later, I said, "Who do you do it for?"

"You mean, do I beat you for you?"

"Yes."

"Kitten, I beat you and hurt you because I like it. I do it for me. But the fact that you respond to it—that's screamingly sexy."

"I don't like pain," I said.

"No one likes pain, Kitten. But you need it." He looked at me. "It's who you are."

Perhaps it was those four, final, liberating words that did it. I found myself on my knees in front of him, kissing his feet. Flooding, rushing, torrential relief.

"Good girl." He stroked my hair, the nape of my neck. I looked up at him. His face was unreadable.

He scooped me up and took me back to bed.

Later.

"Sometimes I think I knew more about myself at five than I did at fifteen or twenty-five," I said.

"Go on."

I looked away, suddenly shy.

He put his hand under my chin, and gently tipped my face toward him. "Go on."

"When I was five, I wrote a letter to my father asking him to beat me with a belt."

A flicker of lust crossed David's face. "Go on."

"I have a feeling the letter was in crayon. I left it for him on his dresser, under his watch. A few minutes later, I got scared and went to take it back. But it was gone." I stopped. I saw myself, a little girl in a nightgown, long hair wavy from having been braided all day, standing on tiptoe to slide a piece of paper underneath a wristwatch.

"What happened?"

"Nothing. He never mentioned it. A few months later, I saw it on his desk, and tried to take it, but he just said, 'That's mine,' and I had to leave it. I don't know if it still exists. I don't know whether he remembers it."

"Did he beat you?"

"No. Of course not. Neither of my parents did. Nor did anyone else. Until you came along."

"Thirty-three years waiting for someone to beat her. My poor, hungry bitch." He smiled a crooked smile.

"I got the idea from a little boy who lived down the street. He told me that his father beat him with a belt if he'd been naughty. Somehow I liked the sound of it. I don't know why. I don't know what I thought it would be like."

I paused. "I also liked the story of *Hansel and Gretel*. Because the wicked witch keeps Hansel in a cage." *I am inside a cage, crouching, naked. Someone, I cannot see who it is, opens a tiny hatch, and reaches in, prodding me, squeezing a buttock. "No, she's not ready," says a voice.*

"I used to lie awake at night, with my fingers in my groin, thinking of being kept in a cage. I have no idea what sort of sensation I got from thinking about it. It wasn't orgasm. I didn't learn to masturbate until years later, not until I was sixteen or seventeen. I don't know what it was, but I remember being fascinated by the way my fingers would smell."

"You'd lie in bed touching yourself—"

"I didn't move my fingers. I just held them there, between my thighs. After a while, I'd bring them to my nose and sniff them."

"While thinking of being in a cage. When you were five."

I nodded.

"Sexy bitch."

Silence. Then he said, "Maria's the same. Always knew she was a bitch, ever since she was a child."

"Where do you think it comes from?" I said.

He shrugged. "A shrink would say it's because your dad smacked you when you were a kid."

I sat up. "But I told you, he didn't smack me. My parents were always really kind. They didn't even yell, not at each other, not at me."

David put his hand on my wrist. "Kitten. I know." I felt my shoulders relax. "Shrinks don't know shit about this stuff," he said.

"So what do you think?" I said.

"What I think is, this stuff didn't start with the Marquis de Sade," he said.

"What do you mean?"

"I mean it's primal. Older than humans." His voice was dreamy. "Dominance and submission—it's what mammals do, Kitten. Ever seen sacred baboons?"

"No. I don't think so."

"They're the ones where the males have big silvery manes," he said.

"Okay . . ."

"You know what they do?"

"No."

"The males subjugate females—enslave them."

I stared at him. How does one baboon enslave another?

"How? What for?"

"For sex."

I've seen it now. In a zoo. A small female sitting between the legs of a bigger, stronger animal. Her head was down. She looked cowed. If she was human, you'd say she was scared and depressed. Every so often, she tried to move away. Each time she did, the male reached out, grabbed her, and pulled her back to where she was. Sometimes it looked matter-of-fact. Sometimes it looked rough.

"What's he doing?" said someone. "She doesn't look like she wants to be there."

No. It was disturbing to watch. A sign on the enclosure explained that a male starts his harem by kidnapping a young female. By punishing her whenever she tries to escape, he teaches her to follow him.

But at the time David was telling me, I hadn't seen any of that.

"Baboon sex slaves? Really?" I said.

He laughed. "Maria read me an article about it."

Maria. Fuck Maria.

He was still talking, "Cool thing is, seems to be genetic. Males that are half sacred and half common baboon can't do it—they don't have the instinct to train the females."

Genetic. I looked at him.

"Do you think—" I said, and stopped.

"Do I think it's genetic in humans?" he said.

I nodded.

"Truth is, Kitten, no one knows. But next time you're in a bookstore, go look at the erotic fiction," he said. "It's all about dominance and submission. Even soft-core romance novels. Why do you think they're called bodice rippers? I think on some level, this stuff appeals to a lot of people." He shrugged. "Maybe most of them never do more than imagine it." Then his voice became so quiet I could hardly hear it. "'Every woman adores a fascist. The boot in the face. The brute, brute heart of a brute like you,'" he said.

"What's that?" I said.

"Line from a poem," he said. "I don't remember who wrote it, but whoever it was—they were onto something. Maybe I'll make you lick my shoes."

But I wasn't thinking about the boot in the face. I was thinking about what had followed. Brute heart? Is that what you have, David?

He rolled onto his side, and ran his fingers along my back, up my neck, into my hair. He twisted his fist, and brought my face to his. He kissed me. As he went on talking, he kept his hand in my hair.

"Human history, Kitten, all that stuff you study, it's just power, sex, and slavery. The big guy has the girls. Pharaohs, sultans, emperors, those guys had hundreds of concubines and slaves."

I saw veils, walls, barred windows, locked doors. Women kneeling, serving. Submitting.

He tightened his fist in my hair, and kissed me again.

"And what guys don't tell you, Kitten, is that power over someone else—it goes straight to your cock."

Silence.

Then he whispered, "The history of women is the history of property."

His face looked greedy as he went on. "Girls were given as presents to the Turkish sultans. They were bought and sold in Greek marriage markets. In Europe until recently, women were the property of their husbands." He paused. "They were owned."

Owned. The word seemed to echo around the room.

When he next spoke, his voice was distant.

"I like ownership," he said. "I think it's a powerful idea."

Ownership. Property. Again, I saw him wave at the darkness and heard him say, "I own everything you see."

He went on. "That time I sat and read while you wanted to be used?"

"Mmm," I said.

"I could do that because I own you," he said.

"You don't own me," I said.

"Oh yes, I do. I've owned you from the moment I punished you for coming too soon. That's when you became my property," he said.

Once again I thought about how my body had leapt toward him, thrilled to him. How it had defied my mind.

He went on, his voice quiet, musing. "I think you own something completely when you can have it and choose not to. Or you decide to lend it to a friend. Or you decide to throw it away."

Throw it away. Property. Throw it away.

I realized I was afraid.

"You scare me sometimes," I said.

"I know," he said. "That's part of what's so sexy. You really are afraid."

"Do you get scared?" I said.

For several moments, he said nothing. Then he said, "I'm afraid I could damage you."

Damage me? How?

If I'd talked to more people, or read more widely, I might have realized he didn't mean he was afraid of hitting too hard, of injuring my body, of putting me in hospital.

It was something else, something worse. A breaking of the spirit.

But I didn't know that.

One afternoon, after lunch, we were lying on the sofa in the sitting room.

"Tell me your fantasies, Kitten," he said.

I flushed. "No, David, come on."

He looked at me and cocked an eyebrow. "Kitten, I've seen you screaming, with clamps on your pussy. I've watched you piss. Tell me."

"Why?"

"I want to know everything about you." He kept his gaze on me, and murmured, "Bitches don't come with manuals. You've got to know what you own."

I was unable to look away. He gazed into my eyes, studying my face.

"Go on," he whispered.

I took a deep breath, snuck up to my place of dark dreams, and opened the door. *I am tied up, legs spread. Men, I cannot see their faces—*

"Rape. Especially gang rape. That's probably my most common fantasy," I said.

"Go on."

"When I was about eighteen, I came across a passage in a book that described soldiers raping a farm girl just before a battle."

Her dress is torn open, her petticoats are around her waist, a line of men waiting, taking turns.

"I used to masturbate to that—still do, sometimes. And I remember, my second year in college, seeing a film that had a rape scene."

A woman held down on a pinball machine. A crowd of men. "You're next," shouts a man, pointing to a fraternity boy. One man so desperate that he pulls the man in front by the hips and takes his place before the man had come. She is trying to struggle. They are fucking her so hard that her head looks as though it's about to be shaken off her body.

"I was terribly upset by it when I saw it—really shocked."

Weeping, knees to chest. Bobby knocking on the door. "Are you okay?" he says, moving to give me a hug. "Don't touch me," I say, backing away.

"Go on," said David.

I paused. *You can't admit this. It's too horrible.*

"But later—" I said.

He smiled a half smile. "I know, Kitten. Later you would imagine yourself in her place."

I shivered. "I've never said any of this before," I said.

"I know."

Silence.

"Have you read—" and he named a book.

"No."

"It has a rape scene in it that stayed with me for a long time."
Eyes half closed, voice far away.

Silence.

"I don't really want to be raped."

"I know you don't, Kitten. No one does. It's the idea that's powerful. Giving up control."

As we'd been talking the sun had shifted. Now our bodies were bathed in the late-afternoon glow.

"And punishment. I knew I liked punishment. I remember there was one night Bobby smacked me a little, just for fun. But I'd spent the evening flirting with another guy, and the smacks felt like punishment—even though he didn't know he was punishing me. It was one of the most arousing evenings we had together."
But it was ages before you could admit it.

"You wanted to be owned," he said.

I shivered.

"It's just in bed, though. I don't want to be dominated in daily life, or work—"

"Kitten. I know." I looked at him. His face was kind. Accepting. I felt my body relax, and found I was smiling a small, shy smile. He pulled me toward him and wrapped me in his arms.

Another day, lying naked in bed in the heat of the late afternoon, listening to the noises of the square below, the people talking and laughing in the cafés, the oinking of the electric pig outside the oddities shop, I said, "I once tried to get Sam to hit me, but he wouldn't."

"It's hard," he said. "It's hard to hit someone you love. It's hard to hit as if you mean it. To hit someone until they cry. That shit's difficult." Was it? He didn't seem to find it so.

"How did you start doing it, David?"

He rolled over and looked at me. "Ever since I can remember, I've known that sex is about power," he said.

Outside, a chair scraped. "Oink, oink, oink," said the pig.

"But in the beginning, I wasn't sure how to get what I wanted. My high school girlfriend, Amy, we had a lot of sex, but it was all very sweet. We read books like *ESO—Extended Sexual Orgasm*, and I worked hard to try and make her come.

"It was great. When we had a free period, we'd get in my car and go to my folks' place, fuck like rabbits, and race back. Do you know how cool it is to sit in calculus class with your fingers stinking of your girlfriend's cunt?"

He paused, and I could see that, for a moment, he was back in high school, sniffing his fingers while the teacher discussed an equation. "Yeah, so, anyway," he said, "Amy and I broke up at the end of high school, but we stayed friends and I went to visit her at the end of the first year of college—she was at school in Chicago. One of her roommates wanted me to tie her up."

"Tie who up? Amy?"

"No, the roommate. So I did. I tied up her up with the phone cord. Then I turned her over and took her asshole. She was screaming and crying. But afterward she was so happy! She loved it. And that's when I realized that there was a market for the stuff I thought about. That there were women out there who wanted to be taken, who wanted a man who didn't ask."

He paused. "Did I ever tell you about Lisa?"

"No."

"I fucked her the day I met her." He smirked. "She and her family lived in this crazy big house in Santa Barbara. Her room was so far from the kitchen that she had to commute to breakfast. It was huge, her room, with this fancy en suite bathroom that had marble everywhere."

Outside, someone coughed.

"We went to her room. I fucked her pussy, then I turned her over and took her asshole. She was screaming!" He paused. "Afterward she sat in the shower and cried for three hours. It was pretty fucking sexy."

I winced at the enjoyment in his voice. "What happened?" I said.

"We went out for a year," he said.

A year? I guess he was right: she liked it.

He was still talking. "We did some extreme shit. One time I left her tied up for four hours. I came back and fed her ice cream, and she puked." He laughed.

Four hours?

"When she got engaged, she called me and asked me to teach her fiancé how to count for her."

"Did you?"

"No—I couldn't do that. What a way to make the guy feel like a loser."

"David?"

"Yes, Kitten."

"How did you start counting?"

He rolled onto his side and smiled at me with the air of a proud inventor.

"I've never read it in a book, or seen it in a movie. It just came to me one day." He paused. "In college, senior year, I was fucking this little blond chick. One day, I decided to make her beg to come. She went crazy, she loved it. That's when I knew I had something." He smirked. "It's been many years since a woman I was with has come without my permission.

"But then I wanted to add something—for the good girls, the A-students, the ones who've always worked hard to please. Like Lisa. Like you, Kitten."

"That's when I started counting. And"—he cocked an eyebrow—"punishing violations." I felt my body shift toward him.

"Does it work for everyone?"

"No. Just the good girls."

"Why did you think it would work for me?"

He laughed. "I didn't think it. I knew."

"But how?"

He smiled his half smile again. "Kitten. I see you."

Silence fell between us. The sounds of the outside world, which had disappeared for a while, came back into the room. Someone's stereo was playing schlocky music, a voice kept singing "It's wonderful, it's wonderful" in English.

At last the voice stopped. The pig seemed to have retired for the night. A pigeon settled on the balcony outside the bedroom, and a light, warm breeze caressed our bodies. The light was starting to fade.

"Tell me, David. What are your fantasies?" I said.

"I'm living one of mine," he said.

Silence.

Then he said, "Complicated. My fantasies are complicated."

His voice took on a hard, faraway sound. "The girls I want to fuck—" He paused. "Adolescents. Girl-women. They have women's bodies, but their minds are the minds of children. They know how to flirt, but they don't know what it means. I want to rape them, take their virginity, then throw them away like used toilet paper.

"Sometimes there are two of them; I tie one up and make her watch while I rape her friend. I want to scare her before I rape her, too. Sometimes it's a mother and daughter: I fuck the mother, then tie her up and make her watch while I rape her daughter. I want the mother to hear her daughter scream."

Jesus God Almighty. I swallowed, hard, and fought down a cry of revulsion.

I raised myself on one elbow, and looked at him. His eyes were closed. A rush of thoughts roared through my head. I thought of the teenagers we'd seen in the square, and the wolfish expression that had crossed his face. I thought of his stepdaughter. He'd watched her grow, become an adolescent. Again, I heard him saying, "She used to practice flirting on me." Had he fantasized about raping her in front of Maria? My mind cringed.

Then, I had a flash of revelation. "That's why you liked the story of how I lost my virginity," I said.

"It's a sexy story," he said, his eyes still closed, his voice still distant.

It's a sexy story. That's what he'd said when I told him about it.

It was four years earlier. David had come to stay for the weekend and I'd taken him to the theater in Stratford-upon-Avon. During the long drive back to London, the conversation turned to sex. I don't remember how. Did I bring it up? Did he? Don't know. But somehow, for some reason, I began telling him about Matthew.

"I lost my virginity to a real jerk," I said.

"Go on," he said.

"Guy called Matthew. I was seventeen; he was twenty-six. I'd known him all my life. Family friend. His parents were friends with my parents. We used to spend the summers in the same beach place in the Canary Islands."

I changed gear.

"I'd always liked him. He talked to me at parties—even when I was just a kid."

There he is, blond and exotic, a drink in one hand and a ciga-rette in the other, talking of houseboats in Latin America, of sailing from Vanuatu to Australia.

"Once, when I was about thirteen, he rescued me. I was wind-surfing, but I didn't know how to tack. So I was going farther and farther into the middle of a bay. Matthew swam out to me—it must have been a mile or so—and sailed the windsurfer back. I held on and he towed me, too."

Clear calm water; a chubby girl with tousled hair; a strong, tanned man laughing.

"He'd probably wanted to fuck you for years," said David.

"My mother warned me about him. I think he'd made a pass at her once."

Be careful of Matthew, Darling. A beautiful woman in a black dress.

"He wanted to fuck your mother, too. Both of you," said David, almost under his breath.

"I trusted him," I said. "To be kind to me. He wasn't."

Silence. No other traffic on the road. Just us, in a capsule, traveling through the night.

"Go on."

"It started the summer I was sixteen. A group of us had been out having drinks, and Matthew gave me a ride home on the back of his motorbike."

Everyone else has gone. He and I are standing in the parking lot, next to his bike. He is lean, strong, handsome.

He looks at me, his eyes narrow, considering.

The night is muggy. Sultry.

He leans down and kisses me.

I gasp.

Hands under my shirt, lifting my bra, squeezing, kneading, punishing my breasts.

He has none of the fumbling hesitation of the boys I know, boys whose only sexual experiences are masturbation and kissing.

Amazement.

"You have incredible breasts," he whispers. "All the guys stare at them."

A car drives past, and he looks over his shoulder. "I'd better get you home. Here." He puts a helmet on my head and pulls my shirt down. No time to rearrange my clothes, refasten my bra. I get on the bike behind him and put my arms around his waist. The muscles on his back ripple as he kick-starts the bike. I have never been so close to a man.

I glanced at David and said, "When we got to the bottom of the driveway, he parked the bike. He said he didn't want to wake everybody up. But instead of taking me up to the house, he gave me a sly look, took my hand, and led me up onto a grassy bank."

Rough grass, frogs bleeping. He pulls me toward him, takes my breasts in his hands. I am lying on the grass under an old tree.

"Go on," said David.

"He unbuttoned his shorts."

And leans toward me. "I can't fuck you: your mother would kill me," he mutters.

"His penis was erect, and large. I—I had never touched one before."

"Go on."

"He thrust it toward my mouth and said, 'Suck me.'

"'What?' I said.

"'Suck me.'

"I had no idea what to do. I tried to remember what I'd read about fellatio in *How to Make Love to a Man*—a sixteenth-birthday present from my friend Cath. And I dredged my brain for what my friend Jeff had told me, the time we'd discussed it."

"What did he tell you?" said David.

"Keep your lips over your teeth and use your hands as well as your mouth."

"Good advice," said David.

"Yeah."

"What happened?" said David.

"I sucked."

Fighting the urge to gag, trying to remember what I'd read.

"And a few moments later, I swallowed. His body went slick with sweat."

"He didn't come because of you, but because of the situation," David murmured, his voice just audible above the engine of the car.

We were on the motorway now; the road fast and empty.

"So you gave him a blow job—what happened then?" said David.

"He left—set sail for New York." I paused. "Which is where I saw him again, nine months later."

A car passed us.

"That guy must be doing a hundred," said David.

"Yeah."

"Go on."

"I went to visit a friend in New York. I called Matthew; he said he'd take me to dinner one night."

Be careful of Matthew, Darling.

"For some reason, it was important to me not to be a virgin when I got to college."

And rightly. I saw JJ, my freshman roommate, and her friends giggling as they went through the book of freshman photos—my copy—highlighter pen in hand, and writing a scornful neon orange "V" over the photo of anyone they thought was still a virgin. One of the friends pointed at me. "No—she's not," said JJ. Credibility saved.

"So when Matthew offered to show me his room—he was in grad student housing somewhere on the Upper West Side—I said yes. I liked him; I trusted him; I thought he would be kind, and skillful." The words came out in a rush.

"Go on."

Elevators, long corridors, a tiny room.

"He . . . he didn't bother with foreplay. He didn't even turn on the light. He stripped me, pushed me onto the bed, reached into his desk for a condom."

Tearing, ripping, blinding pain. I am screaming screaming SCREAMING.

"He didn't try to be gentle. And he threw me out right afterward."

He shudders, groans, then says, "You can't stay here."

As I dress, he pulls the sheets off the bed, stripping it down to the mattress.

"The sheets were covered with blood. So was the mattress."

So was I. Blood. Gushing blood. Won't stop.

"He walked me back to where I was staying, and said he'd call in the morning and take me to lunch."

Sitting by the telephone, waiting.

Waiting.

Fists tight, mind numb, body bleeding.

Waiting.

"He didn't call."

Crying. *Be careful of Matthew, Darling.*

Bleeding. Trying to staunch the blood.

"I was bleeding for three days."

"It's a sexy story," said David, as we drove through the night.

That wasn't the reaction I'd expected. I glanced at him, but his face was in shadow.

We drove in silence for a while. Eventually, I said, "And you, David? How did you lose your virginity?"

"I lost my virginity in a live sex show in Reno, Nevada. It was crazy. Guys were cheering, they were throwing money."

"Are you serious?"

"Yes."

"How old were you?"

"Sixteen." He paused, then added with a dry laugh, "I think she picked me because I looked clean."

"Did you use a condom?"

"No."

"Did you enjoy it?"

"No." The word was hard, definite.

Silence.

My mind wandered back to Matthew, the aftermath. A train pulling out of New York with a teenage girl huddled by a window, crying. Sofia sitting on a wall at school, legs swinging, offering hugs, advice: "Write to him, tell him you don't understand why he didn't call." My voice, anxious: "You don't think I'm a slut, do you?" Sofia laughing: "No, of course not. I'm friends with Jenny; she's already fucked ten guys." Ten guys? At seventeen?

A letter posted. Running to check the mail. Weeks passing. Hope fading, fading, faded.

"It was pretty damaging," I said. "It was months before I let another guy touch me."

"I can imagine," said David.

Silence.

"Have you ever taken someone's virginity?" I said.

"No." The word was steeped in regret.

I looked over at him. While I'd been traveling through Stratford, the Canary Islands, and New York, he'd fallen asleep, oblivious to the fact that yet another stereo was blaring away.

His face was still. I wondered what it was like to know that what arouses you is to make someone scream in pain.

On his last night, after I'd served him supper, he took me over to the full-length mirror by the entrance to my flat.

"I'm going to let you watch while I beat you," he said.

I looked in the mirror. I saw a small blond woman in a black shirt and a long, flowing linen skirt that's longer at the back than at the front. She's wearing a leather collar, and shackles on her wrists and ankles. No one has told her to put them on: she's put them on to please the man who's standing behind her. He's wearing nothing but a pair of shorts. In his right hand, he holds a riding crop. A long, thin stick protrudes from his back pocket. He looks cruel.

He is cruel.

"Pull up your skirt."

I did.

"Higher. Show me your ass."

I did.

"Beg to be beaten."

"Please."

"Please what?"

"Please beat your bitch."

Slam.

"Again."

"Please beat your bitch."

Wham.

To watch his face as he beat me, to see the cruelty, the intensity, the concentration—I was enthralled.

"Beg for the stick."

I heard myself begging him to hit me with the hated stick.

Oh, it bites. It makes the blows from the riding crop feel like kisses. I am screaming. The stick is tearing into my flesh, painting it with red stripes. Two stripes for each blow—it's as though you're hit with a pair of sticks, not just one—and they come up instantly. My thighs are now a mass of stripes. I look as though I'm going to enter a zebra look-alike contest.

But I don't want him to stop. I want him to go on forever.

Somehow, each blow is thrilling, bringing a pulse of ecstasy alongside the agony.

I am entranced.

The insides of my thighs are wet.

He alternates: stick, riding crop, stick, riding crop. I beg and say thank you and beg and say thank you and beg and beg. Please, please. Thank you, thank you.

He doesn't look at the mirror. He looks at the body he's about to hit. He stands behind me, poised, waiting. Then he strikes.

I cry out. He strikes again.

It is the most intense thing I have ever seen.

He is naked now. Standing behind me, erect. Beating me.

I feel as though I am flying. But I'm not flying. I'm wobbling and holding a skirt hiked up around my waist. For some reason I'm on tiptoe.

"I'll be right back. If you move, I'll give you a beating it will take you the rest of your life to recover from."

I stand there, as still as I can, hardly breathing.

He comes back with black jack.

"Bend over."

"No, David, please."

He takes the riding crop and hits me with a backhand.

I bend over.

He kneels behind me. I scream and shoot upright as black jack tears into my anus.

He shrugs, picks me up, and carries me to bed.

In bed, he holds me, strokes me, caresses me.

"That's something to work toward," he said.

"What is?"

"Black jack in your ass."

"No. I don't ever want that."

I had the obscure sense that I'd disappointed him.

I started rubbing myself against him, like a cat.

"Weren't you going to—" I stopped.

"Going to what?"

"Nothing."

He considered me for a moment.

"On your knees, Bitch," he whispered.

I got on my knees. Pretty dog. As he pushed his cock against my anus, I did my best to hold myself still.

It didn't mean it hurt less. God, it hurt. I cried out.

He was quick. When he was finished, he kissed my neck, my nipples. He kissed behind my ears, the base of my neck. He kissed my mouth. With incredible gentleness. As I lay there against him, I felt—complete.

In the night, as he was sleeping, he pulled me to him and wrapped his body around mine. I smiled, and slept.

THREE

I HADN'T dared speak of the future. I hadn't dared think about it. And in the days that followed his departure, I wasn't capable of thinking about anything much at all. I felt like an island after a hurricane: trees uprooted, roofs blown off, cars thrown into the ocean, boats flung onto land. Wrecked, flattened, devastated. I wandered about town, looking in shop windows but not seeing what was there, forgetting what I'd come out to get. I sat at my desk, but couldn't work. When I went swimming, I hardly noticed people staring at the bruises on my legs; but oh, they did stare.

Silence. Nothing. No word.

The phone rang.

Hands shaking, voice trembling, "Hello?"

But it was my cousin. Or my mother. Or a friend.

One, two, three days pass. And three more.

DAMN IT, DAVID, YOU BASTARD, WHY THE FUCK WON'T YOU CALL ME???

The bruises on the insides of my thighs have just about gone. But the switch marks from the last beating look as nasty as they did at the time. They don't seem to have bruised, they just stay red and angry looking.

The hairs are growing back on my pussy. It looks ragged and ugly, and it itches.

Two more days go by.

The switch marks are still there, still livid. What have you done to me?

The phone rings.

"Hello?"

"What's up, Bitch?"

Happiness! Swelling, rushing happiness.

And so things passed to a new phase.

He sent flowers. Armfuls of gladioli. I had to borrow vases from my neighbors. I had flowers on the table, on the desk, in the kitchen, in the bathroom. Actually, they made the apartment look like a funeral parlor, but I didn't tell him so. He sent books, music, and a bag of caramels. He liked lyrical modern novels about big open spaces—Australia, the Great Plains—and ordinary people. I sucked on caramels and read the books while the music played.

He sent a short story he'd ripped out of a book. Across the top of the first page, he'd written, "When I read this story I thought of you and me. I read it years ago. David."

I don't know who wrote it, or where he got it from. But I know why it made him think of me. It was about a successful, independent woman who wants to be dominated and finally, she meets a man who recognizes what she is.

It was fiercely erotic. Yet it made me shudder, for it was a tale of abandonment, of a woman destroyed when she is dismissed by her master. Again, I heard his voice, "Sometimes you have to be cruel to be sexy," and I felt uneasy and afraid.

He sent a small, cheerful, painted wooden dragon that he'd bought in Mexico while on holiday with Maria. He sent a clothes catalog from a fancy department store. On the outside, he'd scribbled, "This is how I will dress you." Inside, he'd circled dresses, jackets, boots—a red silk dress "for the wedding in Vietnam," a faux-tiger-skin jacket "for being silly," tottering heels "for being sexy," a short black dress "so I can have quick access to your cunt."

Do you really want to be told what to wear?

No. It's ridiculous.

I flicked through the catalog again and imagined him looking at the clothes, evaluating, choosing, picturing me in different outfits. Thinking about me.

Then I saw myself standing naked while he picked out this bra, that dress, this pair of shoes. My skin got suddenly hot, and a pulse of lust rippled through me.

Damn him.

While he was sending titillating catalogs, I was writing poems for him. Digging through an old box the other day, I found a copy of one:

Shall I compare thee to a summer storm?
Thou art more vicious and less moderate:
Rough winds do fade and angry clouds lose form,
And lightning's flash is scarcely worth the wait.
Sometimes too cold the tears of heaven fall;
And too swift such violent passions quench'd.
The livid thunderclaps that so enthrall
Fall still. The land again in sun is drench'd.

But thy eternal menace does not fade
Nor does the fury of thy lust decline.
The lurid welts that by thy whip were made
Sting yet: no need thy lashing to refine.
    A brutal master for a hungry slave
    Who with each stroke such thund'rous raptures gave.

I sent him books, too. And photographs—silly, sweet photo-graphs that I took of myself by holding the camera at arm's length, or using the self-timer. Well, not all of them were sweet. For one of them, I posed naked, my back to the camera, in the "offer yourself" position, kneeling, pulling myself open. I cropped the picture at the neck, in case someone found it. For another, I wore the collar and posed in the mirror, holding the camera so it blocked out my face.

I filled my journal with jottings about his visit. Jottings such as:

He smote and I was smitten! Smitten Kitten!

Or:

By my count, we had sex more than forty times in seven days. How does he do it?

For a moment, I thought of Bobby, how he always fell asleep after he came. For a moment, I conjured him, sprawled on top of me as if I was part of the bed. *He could sometimes manage sex twice a day.* But David—

He's superhuman. No: Superman. I'm fucking Superman!

And I wrote:

Why sex before David was boring
No tension. No mystery. No revelation. I didn't get to know Sam or Bobby better through sex.

With David, it's different. It's two people, totally present together.

Suspense. Mystery. Revelation.

I put the journal away and turned back to the article I was working on. To impress David, I'd arranged to write something for a major newspaper, one I knew he read. An opinion piece about propaganda and modern war.

He called when he saw it. "I opened the newspaper and saw your name, and I thought, wait, I know her! Kitten, I am so proud of you. I want you to give yourself a treat. Go and get a massage; I'll pay for it."

Another time, he called to say they'd got the puppy. "We're calling her Daphne. Wait until you see her: she's beautiful."

"What sort of dog is she?" I said.

"She's a—" and he named a breed I hadn't heard of. "They're hunting dogs. Very obedient, if you train them well," he said, with a laugh. "We're starting her at puppy school at the weekend."

Then he said, "Last night I dreamt about you."

"What was the dream?" I said, smiling, delighted at the thought that *he* was dreaming of *me*.

"We were in a big bed, in a room with glass walls, at the top of a high tower. Looking out, we could see lights of the city all around. You had your head on my chest," he said. "It was really powerful."

For a moment we were both silent. I was about to say something, but he spoke first.

"You remember that night I beat you in front of the mirror?"

"Yes."

"I think about that a lot. I felt very close to you that night."

"I think about it a lot, too," I said. "It was weird—when you were beating me, I felt ecstatic. It almost didn't hurt. But you were hitting hard—I had terrible bruises afterward."

"I know," he said. "It's part of the magic."

One afternoon he called to ask if I could leave Italy and come to California. "If you could come to California, spend some time—it would infinitely increase my happiness," he said.

"I have to be in Italy for most of the fall—but I could come for a few days in October," I said.

"Fantastic," he said. "Hold on, let me get my calendar. Okay. How about—" and he named some dates.

"I'll look at tickets," I said, smiling so much I thought my face was going to break.

The next morning, I passed the shop where the mannequins wore the sexy clothes. *Go in.* No. *Go on.*

I opened the door. Bells jangled. A woman looked up. She looked as if she'd stepped out of an elegant sex fantasy. The cut of her shirt was low, and I could see the small blond hairs in the space between her breasts.

She looked at my baggy trousers, my hiking sandals, and said, her voice bemused rather than critical, "My, you're not very sexy today."

She picked out some dresses for me to try. Some were horrid; they made me look like a cheap hooker. Others—I stared at myself in surprise. "That's very sexy," she said, as I emerged in a black dress with a tiny handkerchief skirt.

"But it's not the sort of thing I could wear to a restaurant," I said.

She laughed. "You won't be going to restaurants. In my opinion, your boyfriend will see it and he'll have you on the bed."

I bought it, heart bouncing with excitement.

Caught up by the mad romance of it all, I rummaged around
and found my old diary, the one my mother gave me for Christmas when I was nine. Then I called him, to read out to him what
I'd written about him as a child.

I still have it. The blue leather cover is battered now, the gold
ink that proclaims FIVE YEAR DIARY is chipped and faded. The
lock has broken. Inside, every day has an entry—just a few sen-
tences, but always something. As time goes by, you can see the
handwriting changing, becoming more assured.

I open this small, battered window into the past.

And I am transported to a school playground. One boy is
tramping round the yard, collecting for recycling the foil trays that
the school lunches come in. He shouts, "Give me your perverted
aluminum!" Another boy is saying to me, "You're so lucky David
Fisher isn't here this year." I am ten, new to the school, new to
Miami, new to America. I have no idea what *perverted* means, or
who David Fisher might be. But everyone talked about him. He
sounded exciting. Dangerous.

I began to be fascinated. Who was this boy? When would I
meet him?

First, I met his brother. He was younger, and still at the school;
one day, we started walking home together. He was an unruly,
precocious, foul-mouthed monster—but a kind monster. He used
to share bags of cherries with me.

And then, on April 2nd, my diary reports:

I SAW DAVID FISHER!!! I was walking home with Pia
when a boy came at top speed in the opposite direction on

his bike. As he passed us he said, "Yeeow." Pia said to me, "That's David Fisher." He was so strange.

A boy with black curly hair zips past on a low-slung dirt bike. On May 5th:

I missed meeting David Fisher by a hairbreadth at swimming because I swam earlier than usual. French was pretty boring.

Then, on May 23rd:

I met David Fisher at a swim meet! He is ugly. He is also much worse than his brother. I came third in breast stroke, last in fly, and second in relay. I had a violin lesson.

But apparently he wasn't that ugly, because the next day I reported:

I'd like to see David Fisher again.

He laughed and laughed when I read him that. But at the next entry, he went quiet.
June 10th:

David Fisher is so mean to his little brother. He'll hurt him just to get what he wants.

I remembered the incident. His brother had a can of soda. David wanted it. To get it, he twisted his brother's arm, wrenching it almost out of the socket; the little boy started to yell and scream. The eleven-year-old me was appalled. Appalled enough to put it in her diary.

I teased him. "I'll photocopy June 10th and send it to your brother," I said.

"Don't do that, Kitten. You'll undo years of family therapy."

"You had family therapy because you were mean to your brother?"

"Yeah." He sounded sad.

"Does being mean to your brother have anything to do with—"

"Being mean to women? No."

"That was just a general mean streak?"

"Yeah. Hey, Kitten—" and he changed the subject.

But the diary entries captivated me. "I saw . . . I nearly met . . . I met him . . . I want to see him again"! Oh, the romance! How could we not be together? My fantasies soared, and I imagined us getting married one April 2nd.

I ignored the bit about the mean streak. I paid no attention to the prim little voice that quoted, "The child is the father of the man," at me.

Stupid bitch.

I booked my tickets to California, and we discussed what we were going to do. Perhaps a weekend in a cabin in the mountains? Or a few days at the beach? And a shopping trip—definitely. "I saw a dress I want to get you," he said.

But the next day, everything changed.

I stood, knuckles white as I clenched the telephone, fighting a wave of nausea, fighting to keep a rasp of disappointment out of my voice.

He was begging. *He was begging.* "Don't freak out on me, Kitten. You're the best thing in my life right now."

He'd just told me we couldn't meet in October. He didn't know when we might be able to meet again.

Maria was sick, he said, perhaps very sick; they didn't know yet. She was going for tests. "I can't see you while she's afraid her body has betrayed her," he said.

"Right. Of course," I said.

That was my chance to walk away.

But he sent flowers and parcels, and long entreating letters. "I crave you with an intensity I have never known before . . . the memory of you takes my breath away . . . we have created something spectacular and rare in the world. . . ."

He begged and pleaded. "Wait. Please wait."

"What for, David? What for?"

The line went silent. Then he said something I'd never thought I'd hear him say. He said, "I love you."

You love me? Do you, David? Do you?

But the days passed. The evening air was chilly now. Still he gave no sign of when we could meet.

I got angry.

"What am I supposed to do, David?"

"I don't fucking know."

"What would you do if you were me?"

A pause. "Wait until a certain date, and then leave."

Waiting is a mug's game. I'd promised myself I'd never wait for anyone.

I waited anyway.

Stupid bitch.

While I waited, he began to dream. Big, beautiful dreams, like enormous soap bubbles glistening in the air. Visions, imaginings, impossible promises of how we were going to lead our lives together.

"I'm going to wrap you in a robe, and cook you breakfast, and feed it to you while you sit on my lap; your legs will be covered with bruises, and I'll kiss little kisses on the back of your neck."

And: "I'm going to teach you to dance salsa."

"But I can't do that wiggly hips thing."

"Give me half an hour with a riding crop and you in nothing but stockings, heels, and a garter belt. Your hips will wiggle."

And: "When I come home from work I want to hear your voice echoing through the house as you beg me to fuck you."

And: "I'm going to decorate your body with sapphires and emeralds. I saw some in a shop window when I was in New York last week. They match your eyes."

And, most devastating of all: "I see you as the mother of my children."

"Do you, David?"

"Yeah." Then, "You'd be a fun mom."

It was torture.

For I wanted them. I wanted those dreams to be true.

I knew they were impossible, wicked, and wrong. I wished Maria no harm; I hated thinking about what this must be like for her, about the effect I must be having on her life, about how I'd feel if I were her and my husband talked to another woman as he talked to me. It was appalling, and I was ashamed. Yet something in me kept hoping, wishing—an imp would whisper to me that David had done impossible things before now; that the whole affair had been impossible, but it had happened; that so far, everything he'd promised had come true.

Stupid bitch.

A voice ran through my head, the voice of a friend, in a conversation several years earlier. It said, "Married men talk big. But then they chicken out." It paused, then added, "They always say they're going to leave their wives. But they never do."

Another, sly voice said, "Remember: he's good at bullshit. Says so himself."

A third said, "He's toying with you. He's redecorating his house. He just bought a puppy. He's settled in his life. Forget him."

I blocked my ears and told the voices to go away.

He would call at midnight, and talk to me for four, five, six, seven hours at a time. Night after night after night. After night. We became lost in each other's minds. We talked of books and music and politics, of places each of us had been to and places we'd visit together. Cities like Paris, Istanbul, Buenos Aires. And secret places, spots that each of us loved. "There's a place I go fishing, up in the hills," he said. "I'd love to take you there; it's so beautiful and quiet." We talked of daily life—his job, the puppy classes, a party he was giving. "I'm going to make mojitos, in your honor," he said. And, "I want to be with you for five or six decades," he said.

Maria disappeared from conversation. "I'm going to dinner in the City tonight," he said.

"Are you going alone?"

Silence.

"No," he said.

"Going with anyone I know?" I said.

Silence.

"Maria," he said.

"I'm going out for dinner tonight, too," I said. "To that place where you fed me chocolate ice cream."

"Who with?"

"A guy from my Italian course," I said.

Silence.

"Are you fucking him?"

Pause. "It's none of your business," I said.

"Are you fucking him? Answer me."

"I did."

"Please, Kitten. Please tell me. Are you fucking other guys?
Are you?"

Silence.

"Answer the goddamn question."

"I haven't gone to bed with him yet," I said.

I haven't had dinner with him yet.

"Ask me again tomorrow," I said.

"Please don't do it, Kitten."

"Why shouldn't I?" I said, suddenly angry.

But I didn't.

Stupid bitch.

Other times, he made me thrill to the sound of his voice, drill-
ing me with the familiar questions and instructions, "What are
you? . . . Offer yourself. . . . What do you say? . . . Please what?
. . . Ten, nine . . . five, four, three, two, one . . . come, Bitch,
come now!" He could tell by my breathing alone how to pace the
count. I heard his commands so often that even now, years later,
if someone starts to count backward from ten, I start to quiver
and breathe harder. And if someone were to sneak up and whisper, "What are you?" in my ear, I'm sure I would still say, "Your
bitch."

And he fed me dream after dream after dream.

A diet of dreams is poor food, and I grew thin. Thinner than I
can remember ever being. I started to feel as though I was a
character in a fairy tale—one of the ones where every night, you
get taken dancing in a strange and magical place, and every day
you return to the drudgery of normal life, puzzled as to why your

feet are covered with blisters and your shoes are worn through. I became scarcely able to function; my sleep patterns, never good, became wildly erratic. And when I did sleep, I had dreams of a different kind—dark, savage dreams. I would wake to find the bedclothes knotted and wet with sweat, the pillows tossed across the room.

I tried to escape.

I argued with him.

"And then, we'll have my brother round for a barbecue," he was saying.

"But David, that's just a dream," I said.

"Will you stop with that." His voice sounded tight.

"Is it going to happen?" I said.

Silence.

Then, "It could." A pause. "I don't know whether it will. But it could."

I began to yell. "Stop it. Stop tormenting me with these things you know I want and can't have. Stop it. It's mean. Leave me alone. Let me get on with my life."

I unplugged the telephone and went on dates with other men. But these men were pale and flimsy and dull. They could not compete with this man who wasn't there.

My body took trips, visited friends, went on adventures—weekends in Trieste, Paris, and London, wine tasting here, exhibitions there. But my mind stayed stubbornly in the apartment, reliving beatings and pleasures and laughter, building incredible illusions of the future. Reality was unreal; unreality became thickly tangible.

One morning in November, I looked around and realized: I am falling apart. Bills lay unopened on the table, food was rotting in the fridge. I hadn't followed up invitations to give lectures or write articles. I was having problems in Italian—the classes were in the morning, and after spending all night on the telephone, I often slept through them. Phone calls from friends went unanswered. I hadn't even seen Gio when he'd come to Milan; he'd called and said, "I want you to meet Beppe, my new man. Let's all go and have dinner." Not wanting to miss David's call, I had pretended to be busy.

It was days since I'd done anything social; I'd become a hermit, talking only to a voice, a voice that belonged to someone I never saw, might never see again.

I had to get out of it.

So I booked tickets to California: I would go and say good-bye and stride out of his life forever. I bought expensive new clothes—a miniskirt, a sexy sweater, a bra, a handbag, shoes. I arranged a car and found out how to get to his office. But at the last moment, in a snatch of sanity, I saw I was fooling myself, that I did not want to say good-bye, that I hoped if I appeared before him he would realize he wanted to be with me—*with me, damn it, with me*— and I returned the clothes to the shops and canceled the trip. Instead of getting on a plane, I drove to Rome to see Gio, and meet Beppe.

As I came through the door, Gio wrapped me in a huge hug; his body was warm, his gentle bigness, comforting. Beppe and I kissed hello. As I took off my coat, Gio looked at me, frowning, and said, "You're too thin, you need a haircut, and your clothes don't fit."

I cracked.

"I've fallen in love," I said.

"Ah!" Gio looked interested, pleased.

"He's married," I said. "And he lives in California."

"Mamma mia!" he said.

I explained the situation as though I were giving the synopsis of an opera—girl adores boy since childhood; boy gets married to someone else; boy finally notices girl; they fall in love; boy's wife falls sick. I left out, "Boy beats girl and girl begs for more," and finished with, "He won't see me, but he wants me to be faithful to him."

Beppe burst out, "He wants you to be faithful to him? Faithful to what? If he won't see you, there's no relationship here. There's nothing for you to be faithful to."

He's right.

Gio made a face. "I think it's disgusting," he said. "He knew what you felt about him: he knew that in becoming your lover he would unleash something powerful."

He paused, then said: "His wife will do everything in her power to keep him. She will become sick—many times, if necessary. She will even die, if necessary. Forget him. I don't want to talk any more about David. It's finished." He waved his hand as if dismissing a servant. "Now, *Dolcezza*, tell me how you find life in Italy."

Somehow, that calmed me. We laughed and talked and ate and drank. Gio teased me about the silly mistakes I made in Italian—I asked for *succo di pesce* (fish juice) instead of *succo di pesca* (peach juice)—and by the end of the evening, I was beginning to feel better.

The next morning, as I was leaving, Gio kissed me and said, "The only chance you have is to say no yourself. Do not let him say no to you. Then the situation will be irretrievable."

Right. Definitely right.

I covered pages with scrawling injunctions: *Walk away, walk away, walk away, you have to forget him, forget him, this is hopeless, no good, please please forget him, he's hurting everybody, you, himself,*

Maria, you have to walk away, walk away, walk away. Walk away, you stupid stupid fucking bitch, walk away.

Yet always, in the end, the cravings would get too great and I would plug the telephone back in and thrill to the furious, jealous messages, threatening and entreating and begging me to stay faithful to him. *Are you fucking other guys? Are you? Every day I wake up afraid of losing you. I want you to wait.*

Wait? For what?

"Tell me what I'm waiting for."

"You're waiting for everything."

"What does that mean? Write to me, tell me why I'm waiting. Explain to me how we can be together."

"Of course."

But the letter didn't come.

And still I waited.

Stupid bitch.

The day before I was due to fly to Vietnam for Kim and Paul's wedding, a letter with a California postmark landed on my doormat.

I tore it open.

It said nothing. Platitudes, equivocations, banalities. "You make me laugh . . . I love you . . . I love Maria . . . I don't know how to love two women . . . I am confused . . ."

Goddamn you, David, goddamn you.

I took the Gates of Hell mug and smashed it on the floor. I rounded up the other presents he had given me—the books, the compact discs, the empty caramel packet, the joyful dragon, the clothes catalog, the collar—and put them into a box at the back of my closet. I didn't want to see them. Especially not the dragon. One of the books fell open as I put it in the box, and I saw the inscription he'd written. *For my beauty who for so long was sleeping.* I wanted to tear it out, tear it up.

But I didn't. I packed my suitcase and went to bed.

At three A.M., the phone rang, shredding the quiet.

It could be only one person. Three A.M.? How dare he? He knew I had an early flight to catch.

He didn't wake me, though. I was awake already, restless and fidgeting, twitching from one position to another and kicking at the sheets.

Angry, tired, frustrated, and miserable, I erupted at him. At last.

I told him I was sick of feeling like a tomato.

"A tomato?" he said.

"Yes. A tomato. In a market. Being picked over, inspected, rejected, and left to rot. Look, I wanted to spend my life with you. I'd have given anything for this to have worked out differently. But it hasn't, and I'm through, David, I'm through."

"But—"

"David. This is over. Good-bye."

SILENCE

Dear Gail,

What a shame you couldn't come to Kim's wedding. It was a beautiful ceremony, Kim looked fabulous, the guests were friendly and fun—lots of single men, and women!—the food was delicious, the dancing, raucous. Vietnam has an incredible energy—you see families of five going by on a single moped, everywhere you look people are playing games of one sort or another. . . . The bus tour is amazing; every couple of days we all pile into what looks like an old school bus and go to a new place. . . . While we were in Hanoi, I visited Ho Chi Minh in his tomb, he looks very well, much healthier than many living people. . . . Now we are in the old Imperial capital, Hué; yesterday, a group of us rented bicycles with no brakes, and pedaled off to visit

some of the tombs on the outskirts of town. . . . I bought a
conical hat. . . . I hope you'll come and visit me in Italy
soon. . . .

I found this the other day, tucked into the back of a guidebook. I
think I sent it; what I have looks like a draft.

Reading it now, I'm struck by how . . . enthusiastic I sound.

I'm also struck by how little it reflects the holiday I was actually having.

It gives no hint of how hard it was to watch the wedding, to
hear Paul stand up and say, "Kim, I love you. You are my life." I
thought of David's letter, *I don't know how to love two women. I*
am confused, and I dug my fingernails into my palms to stop myself from crying.

It gives no hint of how small things kept making me think of
David. The carved dragons that grace the roofs of the tombs outside Hué. An offer of a mojito at the hotel bar. The sight of someone reading one of the books he had given me.

How lucky it was that phone calls were so expensive; otherwise,
I might have succumbed. Particularly in the first days of the trip,
when I felt that my face was like a mask, twisted into a smile that
had no relation to the feelings underneath.

The letter also says nothing about Cesar. How, in the days
after the wedding, he had begun courting me, paying attention
to me, making me laugh. How I was starting to like him, to look
forward to seeing him at breakfast, to walking with him on the
tours we were taken on.

I watched as he went up to the bar. He was taller than David,
and leaner. But he had the same dark curly hair; perhaps that's

why I wanted to run my hands through it. And he had the same cocky self-assurance.

And the same kind of belt.

What would he be like in bed? Would he be able to count for me? Or—?

What would I do if he tried to seduce me? Would I let him? Should I?

Ten days since I heard David's voice.

I am okay when I am with other people, but when I am alone—it is hard.

Hard to believe it is really over. But it is. It has to be. Could not go on as it was.

Forget about David forget about David forget about David.

But how—how do I find someone like him? Do I place an ad in the newspaper, "Bitch seeks owner"? "Sexy wildcat needs taming"?

How can you tell if someone likes these things?

Does Cesar?

"Say 'please,'" said Cesar, raising an eyebrow.

"Please," I said, smiling. *Maybe—?*

He handed me a slice of papaya and, as he licked his fingers, talked of coming to visit me in Italy.

Please.

Dancing. Cesar is close to me. He smells slightly of sweat. It's sexy. The neck of his shirt is open, and a few of his chest hairs are sticking out. That's sexy, too.

Now he is close to me. So close he is almost touching. He looks at me. His eyes are full of desire.

I like that. My body begins to respond.

Now they are handing out glasses of champagne. It must be nearly midnight.

Voices begin to count. "Ten, nine, eight, seven."

I found that I was breathing harder.

Oh no. Stop this.

"Six, five, four." I want to mutter "please." I can feel the arousal. I'm going to come.

David, what have you done to me?

David. Please.

David—

"Three, two, one—Happy new year!"

On "happy new year," Cesar planted his lips on mine. I couldn't help it. I moaned as I came.

He thought the moan was all because of his kiss.

He pulled me into the shadows, and kissed me again.

"Come on," he said, taking my hand. "Let's go."

He starts to undress me. Slowly. Gently. He kisses my neck. He strokes my hair.

Oh dear.

I know what's going to happen next. In a moment he's going to move his hand down and start feeling my breast. Then he'll try to undo my bra.

Yup.

What should I do? Put myself in the pretty dog position? Ask him to beat me with his belt? Start begging?

"Please," I murmur.

He stops what he is doing and looks at me. "Please what? What is it that you want?" he whispers.

Oh no!

I guess he's going to think it's weird if I say "Please fuck your bitch."

Probably even "please fuck me" would be too much.

"Please kiss me again," I say, with a smile. I start to unbutton his shirt.

I feel like an actor, going through the motions of a play I've acted in too many times before. I know what I am supposed to do; and I do it because I am supposed to, not because I am present, not because I want to, not because I am caught up by what is going on.

Now I am unbuckling his belt. I suppress the urge to pull it from the belt loops and present it to him.

Now I'm taking off his trousers.

Now we're lying on the bed, caressing each other.

Apparently he's not the sort of guy who talks.

Two people, naked, wrapped in each other's arms, yet remote from each other.

I decide to get it over with. *Assuming he is more like Bobby than like David—if you go down on him, he'll be out of action for the night.*

I kiss his belly, his thighs. He smells of soap.

I take his cock into my mouth. He tastes of soap. I imagine he's David, and tickle his balls.

He's quick.

"Wow. Thanks," he says, lying sprawled on the pillows. He pulls me to him. I put my head at the crook of his shoulder, wrap my legs around his, and pretend to fall asleep.

Later. He is caressing me.

"What do you like?" he says. "Tell me what makes you really wet."

What do I say?

How do I explain?

Is it even worth trying?

"Oh—" I say.

"Tell me," he says. "It'll turn me on."

I like total sex.

I want you to take command.

I want you to beat me, and count for me.

I don't want to know whether I'm going to be hit or kissed.

I want you to be someone else.

I tried to explain.

It was a disaster. Eventually, I said, "What I mean is, I like putting myself in someone else's power."

Silence.

"I don't get it," he said. "You'd be in my power if you were the passenger in my car."

I thought about it for a moment. "You've got the wrong relationship," I said. "It's not the passenger. It's the car. You take her out, you drive her as hard as you can, and afterward, you clean her, polish her, and admire her. That's what I want. I want to be the car."

He was leaning on his elbow, looking at me, frowning.

I thought of David saying, "Kitten, you can always tell me what you like."

I suppressed a sigh.

How am I going to find someone like David?

"Don't worry—it's not a big thing," I said, hoping I sounded convincing. "Perhaps I'll be able to explain it better when you come to see me in Italy."

Soon after that, I kissed him good-bye and went to my room to pack for the journey home.

TWO

FOOTSTEPS. I jerked awake, and listened.

Someone is in the passage outside. Is it him?

No.

Yes. The someone has stopped outside the door. The key is sliding into the lock. The handle is turning.

The door is opening.

It's him.

I struggle to sit up.

"David," says my voice. (Did it tremble? A little.)

I gulp.

He says nothing. He comes into the room pulling a suitcase. He doesn't switch on the light. Though the room isn't fully dark—there's a dim glow coming from the street—I can't see the expression on his face. He shrugs off his coat and comes to the side of the bed.

He unzips his fly, and pulls my head down to his cock.

It's hard.

My forehead rubs against his sweater, my nose against the zipper.

He says nothing.

After a while, I take my mouth away from his cock, and start to undress him. Sweater, shirt, T-shirt fall to the floor. His back is warm and smooth and strong. He steps out of his shoes, unbuckles his belt—I hold my breath, but he doesn't pull it out of the loops— and lets his pants fall to the floor. I strip him of his underwear, put his cock back in my mouth. I run my fingers lightly across the backs of his balls, as though chucking a chin, as he taught me.

My body craves him.

I get on my knees and, in silence, pull myself open to offer myself to him, as he taught me.

He climbs onto the bed and fucks me slowly. He convulses in pleasure—I can see it, he is above me now, looking down at me—then puts his arms around me and falls asleep. All without saying a word.

It feels like a dream.

But it isn't. He is beside me, here in New York, sleeping. I put my nose against his neck and breathe in his smell. I kiss his neck. Little kisses. He'll never know they were there—but they were.

I am relaxed now. But I can't sleep.

There is so much I don't know. I'm still not sure it was right for me to come.

An hour after I'd got home from Vietnam, the telephone had rung. I'd just stepped out of the shower.

"Hello?"

"Happy new year, Bitch."

No. Not now. Not when I haven't slept for twenty hours.

"David—"

"Did you have a good trip?"

"Yes, but David—"

"Can you meet me in New York in two weeks?"

What?

I stared out at the piazza. Why does he have to do this now?

"No, I told you, David, it's too late. We're through," I said.

"So I'm ending a marriage for nothing?" he said, his voice bitter.

Ending—?

Oh God.

When I'd put the phone down, I'd stood without moving for some time.

Is he serious?

Is this what you want? Do you want to be with him?

A siren outside brought me back to the here and now of New York. I turned over, and looked at David. He was still sleeping, his face slack, his mouth slightly open. He looked vulnerable. I found myself wanting to protect him.

In the morning, I woke to find him kneeling between my legs, fucking me. When he saw I was awake, he said, "What are you?"

"Your bitch."

"Beg to be beaten. Because that's what we do with a bitch. That's what you're for."

"No, David, not yet. Please. After breakfast."

He looked at me. And reached over the side of the bed, into his suitcase, and took out a stick. It wasn't the pale one he'd hit me with before. This one was thinner and had bumps every couple of inches or so. It was more flexible, too. Being hit with it was like being hit with a knotted whip. I bit the pillow to muffle the screams.

"No, stop, please."

"By the end of the week, I won't have to tell you: you'll be begging me to beat your pussy, to beat your tits."

"No."

"Yes. What are your tits for?"

I say nothing.

Wham.

The new stick is more savage than the old one. It feels as though it's cutting open the skin on my legs.

"Bitch, what are your tits for?"

"Looking pretty."

He laughed. "No. They're for torturing." He ran the stick over one of them, almost caressing it. "Shall I show you how?"

I held my breath.

He pursed his lips. "No, I think I'll save that for later. I think I'll keep beating your thighs instead. Bite the pillow."

He circled my waist with his hands and said, "Kitten, you've lost weight. I like thin women, but you're too thin."

He was heavier than when I'd last seen him. Not a lot, but enough to notice. As a result of my loss and his gain, he was almost exactly twice my weight. "You're so little I could bench-press you," he said.

"Don't be ridiculous!" I said.

He lay back on the bed, and put out his hands like stirrups. "Climb up," he said.

I laughed, and put one foot into each hand. I rested my hands against the wall to steady myself. He pushed. His arms straightened, and I rose, astonished and giggling, into the air, my head almost touching the ceiling. As he lowered me back down, he winked. "I guess a lot of guys would go to the gym if they could stare into a pussy while they did weights," he said. Laughing, I fell on top of him and tried to tickle him.

"You want to fight?" he said. "Is that what you want? You're going to lose, Kitten. I'm twice your weight." He rolled over, pinning me beneath him. Suddenly, I was helpless; my efforts to escape, futile.

He smiled and took my head in his hands and kissed me kissed me kissed me. Small kisses on my neck, my forehead, my ears, my mouth. I stopped struggling and kissed him back, adoring the sensation of his body crushing mine, losing myself in his strength.

Later, he said, "Let's get dressed and go out. Time to take a walk."

The other day, I found some photographs from that week. A picture of the two of us, in winter coats, standing in front of the hotel. Look how we're smiling! And here's a picture of us behind an enormous pastrami sandwich, a kind of pastrami mountain. He looks startled; I look horrified. I don't think I managed to eat even a quarter of it.

Oh, what a week! For we were in New York! Glamorous, frenetic New York!

And it was his city.

"Let's go downtown; I want to show you where I lived when I spent a summer here in college. Just around the corner there's a place that makes incredible burgers, we can go there for lunch," he said.

"I know this amazing bagel place; let's go there for breakfast," he said.

"Hey, Kitten, let's go down to Union Square, there's a place that makes sensational tiramisu."

I remember, we took a taxi back from Union Square. We sat in the back of the cab, his arms around me, laughing and chattering. The driver, a big, friendly woman, told us we were the happiest couple she'd seen in weeks.

And we went out in the evenings, a young couple about town. One night, after dinner, he took me to hear jazz in a little basement bar. The waiter came and I ordered a Jack Daniel's, no ice. He ordered Tia Maria. My ruffian drinks sweet girlie liqueurs? I looked at him in surprise. And we listened to the saxophones and he told me about being in New York as a student.

"I wore black, and hung out with the artsy crowd. I read existential philosophers during the day and worked as a bartender at night."

"A bartender?"

"Yes, in a supertrendy joint." He laughed. "I was fired."

"Why?"

"For not kissing the asses of our snotty customers."

Another night, about halfway through the week, I took him to the opera.

He had been enthusiastic—when I suggested it, he said, "Let's go to two!"

"Oh, but we don't have much time together. Let's just go to one," I said.

Even one was a mistake.

There we are, coming into the opera house. He's wearing a

suit; it fits him well. I'm wearing a black dress, black stockings, black heels. Would you guess, from looking at me, that I'm not wearing underwear? No, I didn't think so. But I'm not. That was his idea. Of course.

I'm excited. I haven't been to the Met before. Look at the throngs of people! Look at the heavy curtain, the tiers of seats! I give the tickets to the usher—yes, I bought them, this is my present to him. They cost more than I can really afford, but so what? We're in the center of the circle, it's a wonderful view of the stage.

The opera house is full now. The lights go down, the crowd hushes, then claps for the conductor. The first notes of the overture spill into the silence. I'm going to enjoy this.

No, I'm not.

His hands are pulling my knees apart.

Stop it. Please.

I shake my head. He pays no attention. I lean over and whisper in his ear, "Not here, not now. Please, David."

I try to close my knees. His hands yank them apart again.

"Do as you're told, Kitten. Or—" His voice hisses in my ear.

Someone behind us says, "Shh."

Damn it.

What do I do? I can't sit here struggling with him, spoiling the opera for everyone else.

Go with it. You don't have a choice. You won't win. If you fight him, it'll only be more embarrassing.

But why does he have to do it here, now?

I shifted, and bit my lip.

The curtain is up, and one of my favorite arias has begun.

But I'm not listening. I'm sitting with my legs spread, wishing that his hand wasn't massaging my thigh, working its way higher and higher. I try to twitch my dress down, so it at least covers the tops of my stockings. His head turns slightly in my direction; his expression is threatening. He keeps one hand on my leg; with the other, he twitches my dress up again. The tops of my stockings are showing.

He pushes his fingers into my cunt.

I try again to stop him, to move his hand. But he just digs his fingers in deeper, probing, pushing, hurting. On stage, a nobleman is preparing to disguise himself as a student.

The woman next to me nudged her companion, and they both stared at my legs, David's hand. I saw her lean over and whisper to her companion.

At the interval he asked, "What's the point of opera?"

At the interval, the people sitting next to us disappeared and did not come back.

Oh God.

Maybe they're from out of town. Maybe they'd been looking forward to this for months.

As the lights went down for the next act, David was talking, bemoaning the absurdity of the plot and the lousy standard of acting, but I wasn't listening. I was imagining the people next to me going to the box office to complain. "There's a couple in row E—" and the startled porter stammering, his voice hushed, his eyes bulging, "I'm sorry, Madam, they're doing what? Here?"

Of all the strange things that happened during that time, this incident now seems to me one of the strangest. How often have I been to the opera, the theater, or some other night out? And how often has someone next to me had her skirt hiked up, and her cunt fingered and groped?

Never.

But at the time, I didn't think it was odd. Embarrassing, yes. Uncomfortable, certainly. Vulgar, absolutely. But odd? Not really.

What happened to you?

When we got back to the hotel, he sent me up to the room alone. "When I come up I want you ready for me. Don't undress. Put on your collar."

I knew why he wasn't coming with me. He was calling Maria. I heard him while I was waiting for the elevator.

What's going on?

I sat on the bed, propped up against the pillows, in my fancy dress, legs splayed, like a doll. My reflection stared anxiously back at me.

You have to talk to him.

But he didn't appear. And didn't appear. *WHERE IS HE?*

After an hour, the key slid into the lock.

He came into the room and looked at me.

"When I was thirteen, this is what I wanted for my birthday."

"It is?"

"Yes. A beautiful woman I could do anything I wanted with." He rummaged in his suitcase and pulled out a small glass dildo that was shaped like a torpedo.

Tense. Anxious. Unable to restrain myself. "David, what were you doing downstairs?"

"Keeping you waiting."

"No, really. Please?"

"Making some calls."

"Who to?" I sound plaintive. Damn.

A look of annoyance. "Maria."

"David—"

"Not now."

Was that the reason he was so brutal? Was that why he tied me up, gagged me with a T-shirt, slid the glass dildo in my asshole, then put the clamps on my nipples? He fucked me as I screamed into the T-shirt. With each thrust, my tits swung back and forth and the chain between the clamps swung with them, tugging on the clamps, tugging each nipple. New pain, all the time. It doesn't dull and throb, there's no chance to get used to it, it's constant change in pain pain pain pain pain.

The clamp has slid off my left nipple. But now it hurts more on the right, it hurts, it hurts oh it hurts, with each stroke it hurts, stroke hurt, stroke hurt, stroke hurt, a rhythmic blinding stroking hurt.

He notices. "Your left tit's being naughty."

Without pulling out of me, he reaches round and refastens the clamp, screwing it tighter. I am convulsing. Bucking like a rodeo horse. He just rides harder.

I don't notice that I'm crying, but I am. Biting the gag, howling. Muffled, rasping howls.

He twists his hand in my hair, pulls my head up, and makes me watch in the mirror.

"Look at me torturing your tits, Bitch. While I'm pleasuring myself, your tits are in agony."

Then he pulled out and jacked off until he came on my face.

"Your face is my come rag," he whispers as he takes off the clamps.

He carries me to the shower. I stumble back to bed, limp, blank. He fucks me again, gently, tenderly, and I whimper and quiver in his arms, responding to him, to his body, without thought, without resistance. "Please?"

"Please what?"

"Please can I come?"

"Ten . . ."

And I am just there, with him, ecstatic in the night.

"I want to decorate your body," he said. "Let's go."

Bracing air, blue skies. Gloved hand in gloved hand, we walked down Fifth Avenue, gazing at the windows.

"Let's go in here," said David, gesturing at a doorway guarded by a large man in a black coat and heavy sunglasses.

In here? But this is a place for oligarchs and their skinny, made-up girlfriends. Surely someone scruffy like me isn't allowed in?

The sunglasses looked in our direction; the black coat moved to open the door. We went in. The floors were white, the walls were white. The few dresses on display were improbable confections of unlikely materials: a pink leather jacket here, a backless dress in fluorescent green there. A beautiful man greeted us, and asked how he could help.

"We're looking for shoes," said David, smiling at me. He pulled me to him, kissed my ear, and whispered, "Today I'm going to spoil my bitch." I smiled up at him. I couldn't remember the last time I'd been taken shopping by someone else. Must have been when I was a child. "You should feel so loved," he whispered, caressing my cheek with his fingers. A small, jeering voice wondered if this is what love is about, but I ignored it.

White boxes, white tissue paper hiding leather of different colors. I took off my coat and rolled my jeans up to my knees so I could see my leg in the different shoes. Strappy sandals, sandals with no straps, short boots, I tried them all. The beautiful man sat at my feet, fastening buckles, tying laces, pulling boots off my feet.

After much discussion, we settled on a pair of tottery heels that had to be tied on with leather laces that crisscrossed all the way up the calf.

"Sexy bitch," David whispered as the beautiful man packed them up.

It was only when we got to the checkout that I realized how expensive they were. Many times more than the most expensive shoes I'd ever bought for myself. I pulled at his sleeve and tried to protest. He leant down and kissed my mouth, silencing me.

Part of me was sickened by the extravagance. Another part was elated. *If he's spending this much, he must be serious about you.*

"Thank you, David," I said, as the black coat held open the door.

He smiled. "You bet, Kitten."

He hailed a taxi. "Get in. I want to get you a dress, too."

"No, David—"

"You're a grown woman, not a student; it's time you had some nice clothes," he said.

Flying down the avenues, weaving in and out of traffic. We pulled up in front of a small boutique.

"I spotted this place when I was here in the fall," he said. "There's one dress in particular I want you to try."

"But—"

"Kitten. I'm looking after you." *Looking after me?* I turned my face to hide a sudden flux of tears.

No black coat guarded this door; a bell jangled as we went in. A small woman smiled at us. "Let me know if you need help with anything," she said.

David went over to a rack, flicked through it, and produced an elegant black dress with a knee-length skirt. "Try this," he said.

It fitted. Snug but not tight around the bust, tapered at the waist, flared at the knee. *How can he find clothes that fit you, but you cannot? How does he do it?*

I came out of the changing room.

He gazed at me. "You look so beautiful," he said. "We'll get this dress," he said to the saleswoman.

As he paid for it and smiled at me, I felt as though I was wrapped in a duvet of goose down, the feathers so light you scarcely feel them, the warmth enveloping but not smothering.

"There's one more place I want to take a look at," he said. "It's a couple of doors down."

It was a jewelry store. He pointed at the window. "I want you to try that," he said, pointing to a gold chain with big, round links. "It used to be a man's watch chain," he said.

A bald man came out from behind a counter of rings and lockets, and fetched the chain from the window display. David fastened it tight around my neck as though it was a collar. A small piece of it hung down my back. "It looks like a leash," he whispered. He looked at me, considering. It was much cheaper than the shoes. But he didn't buy it.

"We'll take a walk around the block and think about it," he said, unfastening it and handing it back to the bald man.

But as soon as we left the shop, we got into a taxi and went back to the hotel.

Thursday afternoon. He still hasn't said anything. Just one more whole day left. Don't want to ruin tomorrow, our last day together.

We're lying in bed, spoons fashion, with me behind.

"David?"

"Yes, Kitten?"

"Oh, David. You know what I want to know. Please don't make me ask."

He sighed.

Silence.

Then, speaking with his face turned away from me, he said, "The moving vans are coming. Maria and I are having a trial separation. We've told my folks. She's staying with a friend while we get her apartment ready. She still stays with me some nights."

Trial separation? That's it? But you said—

But I didn't press. I didn't ask questions.

Why not?

Because he sounded miserable. I gazed at his back, suddenly aware that this man who always seemed calm, controlled—that he was in turmoil.

"I'm sorry it's so awful," I whispered.

He nodded.

"She blames you. I don't," he said, still facing away from me.

"She blames me for what?"

"Having dinner with her, then fucking her husband."

Breathe.

"But David. I asked you at the beginning. You said she was okay with it."

He nodded.

"She was. Then she wasn't."

"When—"

"She didn't want me to come to Italy."

Oh God. But—we got her a present. And you called her two or three times a day.

"I hadn't taken three weeks off work in years, and when I did, I chose to spend the first week away from her." His voice was harsh. "And in the fall, she wanted me to stop calling you."

I stared at his back.

"She felt included before." His voice was agonized.

Included. I rolled away from him and held my knees to my chest.

"Does she know you're here with me now?"

Silence.

"No."

Married men are creeping, furtive.

I bit my lip.

But at dinner that night, he gazed at me and talked of "the outcome we both hope for." And he outlined the months ahead. I would arrange to do some work in California in February; we would meet in London in March. And why didn't we go on holiday in Japan in April? Perhaps in the summer—perhaps I could bring my fellowship to California and we could move in together.

I held my breath and studied his face—the lines on his forehead, the heavy eyebrows, the curve of his nose, the set of his mouth. And I looked into his dark eyes, and smiled.

Hope.

The next morning he gave me the most savage beating yet.

I begged for it.

We were lying in bed. He gestured to his erect prick.

"Get on," he said.

I climbed onto him.

"Please."

"Please what?"

"Please beat your bitch."

He raised an eyebrow.

"Please, David. Please beat me."

He picked up the stick.

Wham, across the flank.

I lift my arms over my head, bringing my breasts up, making them rounder.

"Please. Please beat my tits."

He watches me intently, then raises his hand.

Somehow, it doesn't hurt. And I want more. I'm fucking him, begging him to beat me harder, beat me more.

What sort of ecstasy is this?

He starts hitting my stomach. Again and again and again.

He turns me over.

"Offer your pussy for a beating."

I spread my legs and grab my ankles.

"Beg."

"Please. Please beat my pussy."

Crash. He hits me sideways, across the backs of the thighs, across the lips of my pussy. It bites. I yell. But somehow, the humiliation of it, of being beaten in such an intimate place, is thrilling.

"Again," he said.

"Please."

Rapture.

Afterward, he picked up my camera and took photographs of his handiwork.

I found the pictures the other day. In a sealed envelope, marked CONFIDENTIAL, at the bottom of a box of letters.

They are shocking. What sort of spell was I under to let that happen?

Here's one. It shows a naked woman with pale skin lying on

rumpled white sheets. Her head and breasts are covered by a pillow; her legs are lying together. Her stomach, rib cage, and belly are streaked with welts. Livid, raised, red welts. More than fifty. Each welt comprises three narrow stripes: red, white, red: the flag of the Land of Pain. The welts continue down, licking her crotch, striping the insides of her thighs. The front of her right thigh is a dark smear of old bruises.

Here's another. It's a crotch shot: the legs are splayed open. Welts flame around the curves of the buttocks, down the insides of both thighs, across the pussy. The insides of both thighs are dark with the fat bruises made by a riding crop.

"Show me pretty dog," he had said, and once I was on all fours, he had walked around me taking photos. The buttocks look like bruised fruit. Here, too, you can see how the stick crashed across the lips of my pussy. Both hips are dark with old bruises and red with new welts.

And look at this one. Here you can see my face, and my breasts. My breasts have savage welts across them, too. But look at my expression. I look tired, overwhelmed, stunned. Beaten.

As usual after a savage beating, I was in a daze. My mind had gone blank; the internal monologue was silent. I was just there, in the now, without thought.

"I'm going to show you off at the fetish shop," he said as he put down the camera. "Get dressed. We're going out."

"No, David. Please."

Don't make me go out like this. Please. Can't look after myself. Can't talk. Too dazed. Please. Want to stay here in your arms.

But ten minutes later, we were in a cab heading downtown.

"We're here," he said to the driver. We got out.

The street didn't seem to have any shops. He checked the address on a piece of paper. We stopped in front of a nondescript doorway.

"This is it, Kitten," he said, pushing the door open. "Welcome to Purple Passion. I'm going to get you a corset."

We stepped into a gloomy, cavernous place.

The shop was empty of customers, but crowded with things for sale. Narrow aisles led past racks of whips, chains, dildos, gags, nipple clamps, cock rings, spreaders, swings, cages, books, films, and a huge selection of clothes. Clothes of rubber or leather, maid and nurse uniforms, capes and corsets—the stuff of all the stereotypes. A Styrofoam head wearing a hood leered down from one of the shelves. Bulletin boards advertised parties, classes in spanking, and unusual equipment.

David propelled me through the shop to the back. I looked around blankly. My mind still wasn't working, and I wanted to take a nap. A large, cheerful woman came up to us. "Can I help?" she said.

"Looking for a corset," I mumbled.

"What sort are you looking for? One that covers the breasts, or waist only? Leather? Velvet? Rubber?"

I had no idea what David had in mind.

"Er . . ." I said, and paused.

"Well, if you don't know what you're looking for, maybe he does," she said briskly, looking at David.

"Why doesn't she try on several?" he said, and together they picked out a selection.

The large, cheerful woman led the way to the changing room: a cubicle with a big mirror, a couple of chairs and a small table. It was separated from the rest of the shop by a curtain.

"Do you want to come in, or wait outside?" she said to David.

"Sometimes guys like to watch; sometimes they like to have a surprise."

"I'll wait out here," said David.

I took off my coat, sweater, and bra, then Large and Cheerful helped me into a blue leather corset that covered my breasts. It had ranks of hooks up the front, and laces down the back. She helped me with the hooks, and then laced me in. I didn't like it: the leather was stiff and coarse, and I thought it looked tacky.

David came in and looked me over. He walked around me, appraising. He shook his head. "Try another one," he said, sitting down on one of the chairs.

I wasn't used to having anyone watch me in a changing room. Now I had two spectators, and I felt shy. As Large and Cheerful released me from the first corset, I began to turn away, to try and hide my body, but I caught the look in David's eye, the slight, slow, menacing cock of his eyebrow. I swallowed, and turned back.

Several corsets later, I'm in more of a daze than ever. My breath keeps getting squeezed out of me. Meanwhile, Large and Cheerful is showing David how to lace a corset and they are discussing how long one can safely be worn. "At first, I wouldn't have her in it for more than twenty minutes, half an hour. It displaces the internal organs, you know." Great. "When she's used to it, she could wear it for a couple of hours."

She went on, "Lots of girls like corsets because it makes them feel confined. As if someone is holding them tight." Oh good.

Now they're talking about me. "She's small," says Large and Cheerful, picking up the first of a number of short corsets—the ones that cinch the waist but leave the breasts bare.

"Yes," says David, with a smile.

As Large and Cheerful laces me into a pretty short corset of black velvet, David comes around in front of me, and begins to fondle my breasts as casually as a man fondles a dog's ears.

No.

Please.

I try to pretend I'm not there, that this is happening to someone else.

Large and Cheerful is kindly pretending not to notice; as he tugs my tits, she goes on tugging the laces at the back.

Stop. Please stop.

I try to push his hands away. Futile. I gaze up at him, imploring. He's not looking at my face. He's watching his hands knead my breasts. Twist, turn, pinch. I lick my lips. Now he's holding me by the nipples, and talking to Large and Cheerful. I can't take in what they're saying. I'm rigid with shame.

Now he wants me to try on latex skirts. Tight, tarty latex skirts. When Large and Cheerful goes to get some, he whispers, "She knows what you are—that you're property."

I shake my head. "No."

He smiles. "Yes. She's talking about you as if you're not here."

Oh God. She is.

"She knows you don't talk to property." He pauses, watching my face. "She saw the welts; she knows what they're from. She sells sticks every day that make welts like that. She saw me handling you. She knows, Kitten, she knows."

I shudder. The backs of my knees are trembling.

Please tell me this isn't real.

He decides against the corsets, but buys me a red latex skirt. I didn't like to say that I hated it, that I thought it made me look cheap and slutty.

"I was so turned on I nearly took you right there in the changing room," he said, as we left the shop.

Thank God.

"I think she felt sorry for you," he said with a laugh.

I did, too.

"You were fabulous," he said. "The ultimate bitch. I'm proud to own you."

The ultimate bitch? Where had I heard that before?

ONE

THREE WEEKS later.

"David, let's go back to the hotel and order room service. Please."

"Kitten, don't be silly. You'll love this place. House of Nanking. Best Chinese food in San Francisco."

But it felt wrong.

It was my fault. I shouldn't have suggested meeting on Valentine's Day. Too loaded.

"David, please."

"What's the matter, Kitten?"

"It's just . . . well . . ." *You have to ask.* "Does Maria know I'm here?"

Silence.

"Does she?"

"No."

"What if we run into her? Or one of her friends?"

He laughed. "What's the chance of that? Come on, get out of the car. Fucking you is hard work: I'm hungry."

We walked up the hill. I was hungry, too. And dazed. Too dazed to argue. In no state to be out. I wanted to be in bed, being cuddled.

My body hurt.

An hour before, he had set upon me with, if possible, a new level of ferocity.

He had called to say: "Bitch, I'll be there in ten. Take off your clothes, leave the door to your room open, and get on the bed and offer yourself. I want your cunt waiting for me."

Prop open the door to my hotel room? While I kneel naked on the bed?

But wait. What's more scary? The possibility a stranger might walk in? Or David's rage if I don't do it?

David's rage.

Ten minutes. Time for a shower. Jump in. Hot water pelting on my back. Ahhh. But hurry, no time to linger. Jump out.

He's going to be here any second. Hurry, hurry. Want to have a good Valentine's Day.

The door. Quick. Hmm. How to keep it ajar? I know. I can flip open the security lock. That'll work.

I cracked open the door. Started to flip the lock. A hand reached through and covered mine, pushing it backward into the room. The door started to open.

He was there.

I swallowed. Mouth gone dry.

"Didn't I tell you to—"

"I'm sorry, I was about to do it, I didn't have time, you arrived sooner than I thought." I heard myself babbling.

Silence.

He came into the room. He moved toward me. I backed away. The door closed behind him.

"You know what happens to disobedient bitches, don't you?" he whispered. "Get on the bed." He smiled a small, cruel smile.

I glanced at the building opposite. The roof was level with my window. Two men were standing on it, smoking.

"Please, David. Let me close the curtains."

"No. I want everyone to see what I do to you."

"Please."

"No. Get on the bed. Show me pretty dog. Now."

I knelt.

"David—"

"Shut up. Today I'm going to fuck you as though you're a piece of furniture. I don't want you to move. I don't want to hear a sound. Even if I beat you. I want to use your body in silence."

He didn't bother to undress. He just unzipped his fly and mounted.

Silence. Just the creak of the bed. Hands on my hips, pulling, pushing, pulling, pushing.

He pulled his belt out of the belt loops and beat me with it. My mouth was wide open, I was grimacing, but I did not make a sound.

He threw the belt to one side, grabbed my arms, and pulled them out from under me; I fell on my face. He yanked my arms behind my back and held both wrists in one hand. He knelt astride my prone body, fucking fucking fucking. A fury. Fucking.

I squirmed, turned my head, tried to see his face. I couldn't.

"Now you know what it's like to be raped, Bitch," he whispered. "This is how they do it. Face down. You're helpless. You can't struggle, you can't get away. And if you try to close your legs, it just feels better—makes your cunt tighter. You didn't think it was like this, did you?"

I shook my head. "No."

"No. In your fantasies, you're on your back, you can see their faces." He laughed a hard, mean laugh. "But it's not like that. It's like this."

He started fucking harder harder harder, shaking me as though I was a dusty rug. My head rattled.

He was right. I was helpless.

"Please let me see your face, David."

"No."

Groans. He groans with pleasure.

"Don't move."

I lay where he had put me, face down as he left me, arms falling to my sides, legs splayed.

He disappeared into the bathroom. I heard him turning on the faucet.

Silence. I could feel that he was back in the room.

"That was just the start," he said. "How should I punish my bitch for disobedience?"

I rolled over, sat up. "No, please, David."

He was naked now, but for a shoelace.

"Bitch, I said 'Don't move.'" He came toward me. "Is my bitch a glutton for punishment?"

"No. No. Please." I rolled back onto my belly. It's hard to negotiate from here.

"Should I beat her some more?"

"No. Please."

"Should I take her asshole?"

"No, David, please, no."

"Get on your knees."

I glanced at the roof opposite. There were five men now.

"David, please close the curtains, please."

"No. You're going to put on a show."

I tried to turn my head away, to hide my face.

"Not like that. Head up. Proud bitch."

"David, this is too much—"

"Shut up, Bitch. They all know what you are."

I howled and bucked and struggled as he forced himself into my asshole. "Here's your punishment, Bitch."

I am howling. Sobbing. Whimpering.

"Get dressed. I'm hungry. Let's go to dinner," he said.

"Give me a hug?" I said.

He hasn't said anything about it being Valentine's Day today. I have a present for him. But maybe it's a bad idea to give it. If he doesn't have anything for me.

Keep it light. Don't let the mood get heavy.

He was putting on his trousers, buckling his belt. He came over to me and stroked my hair. I took his other hand, turned it over, and kissed the palm.

He's still wearing his wedding ring.

The sight of it made me angry. *He's supposed to be separated. Unmarried.* I wanted to tear it off, flush it away.

"Come on, Kitten, get dressed." He held out some clothes.

Wish I didn't feel so zonked. Hate going out like this. Want to stay in bed, snuggling.

I stood up. Unsteady. My body hurt.

Don't want to go out. Want to be cuddled.

But now I was dressed, we were in the elevator, we were getting into the car.

"Where are we going?"

He said, "I figured you wouldn't want a big fancy dinner."

Oh?

"So I haven't booked anything."

I knew Valentine's Day was a mistake. He doesn't feel comfortable. It's too much, too early.

"There's a great place I know that doesn't take reservations. We'll go there."

"Happy Valentine's Day, David."

"Happy Valentine's Day, Kitten."

No, he doesn't have anything for me. Okay, I won't give him his present, then. Keep it light.

It was chilly. We were walking up the hill. He put his arm through mine, kissed me, and smiled.

Wish I didn't feel so dazed. Wish we'd gone to his house, like I'd originally suggested.

What if we run into Maria? Or one of her friends? The thought wouldn't go away.

I glanced about. The street was lined with little shops, lanterns hanging in the windows. There were lots of people. Couples, mostly. Laughter and chatter all around.

"Here it is," said David.

The House of Nanking. Throngs of people were waiting outside. We joined them. He kissed me and pulled me to him, his arm around my shoulder. I smiled up at him.

"This place is an amazing business," he said. "They must make shitloads of money. Let's see, they've got about twenty tables, on average I'd guess customers stay an hour, so that's—"

He stopped.

I turned to look at him. His face was closed.

"David? Are you okay?"

Silence.

"David? What's the matter?"

"Kitten, we've got to go."

"What? Why?"

"They just seated Maria's daughter."

What? No. NO!

I stared at him. My mind stuttered. He wants to run away?

"Please, Kitten. It's going to be really uncomfortable for me."
His voice, imploring, begging, seemed distant, remote.

Keep it light. Pretend you don't care. Pretend, pretend.

"Yes. Okay. Of course. Sure," I said, as brightly as I could. And
we turned, and kept walking up the hill.

"I know where we can go," he said. "There's a great place just
around the corner."

I don't seem to be able to talk. I want to. I want to dispel the
mood that has fallen. This is Valentine's Day, for chrissake. We
should be having fun. Gazing into one another's eyes. Smiling,
laughing. Not running away. Come on. Pull yourself together.
Smile. Laugh. Make jokes.

Nothing.

After about five minutes, we arrived at a Lebanese café. The
lights were bright; the shadows, harsh. The place was deserted.

We stood at the counter. "What would you like, Kitten?"

"Er . . . falafel? And a glass of water. Thanks." I craved a glass
of wine, but that wasn't on the menu.

We sat down at a table in the corner.

"Well, that was a buzzkill," said David.

His face looked drawn.

"David. You've got to tell Maria. She's got to hear it from you.
Don't let her hear it from Nina. Please."

"I don't think she saw us."

"It doesn't matter. You have to tell Maria. David, please."

Silence.

I didn't push it.

I should have.

Even now, years later, I feel sick when I think about that night. If it hadn't happened. If we'd stayed in the hotel. If I hadn't been so dazed. If we'd arrived an hour earlier. If I hadn't suggested Valentine's Day. If I hadn't come to California at all. If, if, if— maybe it would all have been different.

At the time, I tried to talk. To joke. To laugh.

I couldn't. I seemed to be looking at the world through a thick fog. My brain seemed to have stalled.

I ate the falafel. He ate whatever it was he'd ordered. He looked small, as though he'd shrunk in the wash.

The silence went on forever.

We got up to go.

"Can you stay tonight?" I asked, as we drove back to the hotel.

"No. Got to get back and walk the dog. I'll pick you up tomorrow around eleven. We'll go get some brunch and then head to my place."

I leant over and kissed him.

"Good night, Kitten," he said.

What a contrast to the start of the week.

The previous Sunday morning I had been in a stall in the public bathrooms of San Jose Airport, taking off my underwear. But shhh! Don't tell David. I'm cheating. He told me to take the flight to San Jose with no underwear on, but I'm taking it off only at the end. I slipped it into the side pocket of my suitcase, and emerged from the stall. I caught my reflection in the long mirror by the doorway. She smiled at me. She seemed to like the effect of the tight black top, the straight black skirt, and the pointy Italian shoes with the bold black straps that crossed in front of my ankle and closed with a zip at the back. They had saucy little kitten heels, my shoes. She and I swept our fingers through our hair, then gave each other a jaunty wave as I walked out of the bathroom, pulling my suitcase behind me.

Of course I was jaunty. The night before he had called me, and begged me, pleaded with me.

"When is the conference over?"

"Next Sunday."

"When do you go back to Europe?"

"The following day—Monday."

"Can't you change your ticket? Stay with me the whole week? I'm good with that."

I was doubtful, reluctant. "A friend is coming to stay with me in Italy next week."

"Can't you cancel?"

I hesitated.

"Come on. I can drop you at the library in the morning and pick you up after work. We can cook together, play tennis together, go to the theater—oh, Kitten, it'll be great."

A wise little voice in my head said, "Don't do it. Don't change your plans—that's a bad idea. You're seeing him in London in two weeks anyway. Better to leave him wanting more."

A bigger, jubilant voice said, "This is your dream coming true! This is the beginning of your lives together! You will go out together, be seen together! You will sleep in his bed! You will be a real couple!"

The bigger voice won. I canceled on the friend, and changed my ticket.

"Good girl," said David, when I told him.

Stupid bitch.

But as I walked out of the bathroom at the San Jose Airport, I was just happy that he wanted me to stay.

A few moments later, I saw him. He was sitting with his legs crossed, his dog at his feet. He was caressing her ears with one hand, holding the leash in the other.

"David!"

He gave me a big smile. It was warm, open, joyous. "What's up, Kitten?"

He stood up, moved slowly toward me, twisted one hand in my hair, and kissed me languidly, deeply.

"Got your stuff?" he asked.

I nodded.

"Let's go. Come on, Daphne," he said to the dog.

She trotted along beside us as we walked out to the car. "My two bitches," he said. "Perhaps I'll put you on a leash, too, and take you out for walks together."

The thought made me quiver, and brought a wetness to my thighs.

I sat in the car, and spread my legs.

"Feet on the dashboard, Bitch."

He started the engine, then reached over to me. His hand traveled up my thigh, higher, higher. He smirked at the wetness. His hand is in my pussy now. He is feeling, exploring, probing, stroking.

He is pleased with me. I am not wearing underwear. And I've shaved off my pubic hair—it took me ages this morning. I'd sat on the edge of the bath, legs spread, with a razor and a hand mirror. And now my pussy is naked, smooth.

"Nice work on that pussy, Kitten," he said, pinching the labia closed as though he was going to zip them shut. He looked greedy, lascivious.

"I'm going to fuck you so hard when we get to your hotel in Santa Cruz. Now tell me what you're going to say in your lecture tomorrow."

When I think back to that afternoon, I feel a rush of happiness. Then comes an ache of sadness.

I see us in a little tacqueria, eating lunch, while Daphne sits outside, waiting. Now—look!—we're dancing salsa on the boardwalk by the ocean. I'm clumsy and slightly behind the beat. David's hips gyrate like a Cuban's. Mine remain stubbornly Anglo-Saxon, rigid and stiff. David is patient, leading firmly but gently. "Just do a little bit each time you have the chance—you'll pick it up." And, "Don't worry about the hips at first."

The ocean is a deep blue, spangled with flecks of sunlight and dollops of foam.

Here we are playing with Daphne in front of the enormous skeleton of a whale. David is training her, rewarding her with dog treats when she does the right thing. "Stay!" "Sit!" "Beg!" "Come!"

I'm jealous. "When is it my turn? I want to come."

"My bitch is greedy," he says, with a laugh. "She's got to learn to wait. Like this."

He turns to Daphne and puts a treat on her front paw. "Wait!"

The dog's nose twitches, her brow furrows, and she stares at the treat. Seconds pass. . . . ten, nine, eight . . . two, one,

"Okay, Daphne!"

She gobbles the treat.

"Good girl," he says, patting her head, fondling her ears.

That day, in my Santa Cruz hotel room that had a view of the pier stretching into the sea, he was gentle with me. Rapacious, but tender. Before lunch. Again, in the mid afternoon, fucking me slowly, beating me tenderly, beating so I gasp but not so I scream. A shout, "You want to see my face, Bitch? Look, Bitch, look now!" and his face contorts in pleasure that seems without end. And now the sun is setting, the seagulls are bobbing on the distant waves, and I am straddling him, facing his feet, rising and falling as though trotting on a horse, a position he likes but from which he never comes, I am playing with his balls, tickling them lightly lightly, rising and falling, rising and falling, his hands are on my hips, suddenly he holds me down, grinds me into him, I can feel him convulsing, shuddering, I hear him groan.

Silence. Stillness. We are a single statue in the last rays of the sun.

He pulls me backward, so I am lying flat against him, my buttocks against his belly, my back against his chest, my head against his neck. He wraps his arms around me, his arms crossed on my chest, holding me by the breasts.

Breathing together, into the silence. Chests rising, falling, rising, falling together.

After a while, he speaks. "I come so hard with you, now. I've never known anything like it."

I quiver with pride and find myself smiling inanely at the twilight.

Later, he said, "Hey, Kitten, what's your schedule like the rest of this week?"

"I've got meetings in Santa Cruz until Friday. I don't think I'll be able to get to San Francisco until late Friday night. I've got meetings in the City all day on Saturday—but we could do something Saturday night."

Valentine's Day.

"Are you free? Maybe we could spend the evening at your place?" I said.

He nodded.

"Saturday," he said slowly. He gave a dry laugh, more like a bark. "Isn't that Valentine's Day?"

I nodded, and looked at him sideways, playing coy. I couldn't read his expression.

Why, why, why? Why didn't I just leave it, wait to see him the day after? Greedy bitch. How could you be so dumb?

On my hotel bed in San Francisco with no view of the sea, just of a roof where five men had watched David fuck me a few hours before, I skipped the rest of the recollections of that night of gentle pleasure in Santa Cruz ("Ten, nine . . . two, one, come, Bitch, come now!"), and ground my fists into the pillow. Again and again I heard David say, "They just seated Maria's daughter . . . we've got to go . . . daughter . . . I don't think she saw us. . . ."

I lay awake for a long time.

When he came to pick me up the next morning, he looked awful. As if he was about to be sick.

"Are you okay?" I said.

"Yeah."

"What's up?"

"We'll talk about it once we've eaten," he said.

Uh-oh.

The restaurant was packed. He had a word with the maître d'. "It's an hour to get a table," he said. Huge trays of dim sum whizzed past us leaving delicious, hunger-making smells in their wake. "Or we can get takeout." He pointed to a counter in the corner, where Styrofoam boxes of food were being dealt out like cards in a casino.

"I don't think I can last an hour. Let's get takeout," he said, and marched to the counter. I followed.

Wish I felt more compos mentis. Body still sore. Mind still numb. Tired, too. Come on: smile! That's a girl.

He ordered steamed buns, and dumplings, and pot stickers, and goodness knows what else, and we staggered to a bench bearing twin towers of boxes.

"We can't possibly eat all this!" I said. But we did.

Afterward, he looked better.

"Let's go," he said.

We got back into the car, and set off toward the highway.

"So what is it?" I said, glancing over at him.

Silence.

He was watching the road. He changed lanes. I waited.

"Maria called. She wants to stay tomorrow night. I can't see a reason to say no."

My stomach balled and knotted. As though I'd been kicked.

You can't see a reason to say no? What about me?

My internal monologue split into a screaming mob.

Don't say anything. Don't. Pretend you don't care. Keep it light.

But he invited you—begged you—to stay for a week. He gave you the impression he was ready for you to be a couple, together, in public. Not fleeing in shame from restaurants, or throwing you out of his house.

He hasn't even said sorry. Or offered to put you up for a night in a hotel.

He's throwing you out. As if you're a toy.

If you hadn't changed your tickets, this wouldn't have happened. If you hadn't trusted him more than you trusted yourself.

If.

I wanted to say, "Of course, no problem." Or, "Okay, I'll go and stay with Gail." But I couldn't. I couldn't say anything.

We drove down the highway in silence, each in a private hell.

He pushed open the front door of the house and carried my suitcase past his bedroom, to the guest room.

The GUEST ROOM? He's not taking you into his bed?

He put the suitcase down. "I wonder where the dog is," he said.

Come on. You've got to dispel this mood.

I just want to have a nap. So tired.

Come on.

I went over to him, and kissed him on the mouth. Hard.

"I need a nap," I said.

"I'm going to fuck you first."

He fell asleep afterward. I couldn't. Too tense. Shoulders knotted. Stomach aching, as though someone was twisting my insides.

Got to talk to someone. Got to figure out what to do.

I slid out of bed. He slept on. I dressed, and tiptoed out of the room.

I'm going to take his car. Got to get out of here. Got to go somewhere I can talk without being overheard.

His keys were lying on the table by the front door. Why does he have so many? What are they all for? It's like the keychain of a prison guard.

I trudged up the hill and got into the car. Christ, it's disgusting. Why is it always so dirty?

I put the key into the ignition.

I can't drive; I can't see. Too many tears.

I leant back against the driver's seat.

First, last night. Now this.

What do I do now?

Stay? Go?

GODDAMN IT.

Why why why?

I realized I was pounding the steering wheel with my fists.

Calm down. Breathe.

But what do I do now?

If only I hadn't changed my ticket. Why did I let him talk me into it?

If only I hadn't come to California at all.

If-if-if-if.

I looked around the parking lot. How can the sun be shining? Why are the birds singing?

Do I call Gail, and ask if I can come and stay?

Do I ask him to put me up in a hotel?

Do I go home?

I can't call Gail. What am I going to say? "I've been thrown out, can I come and sleep on your floor?"

It's pathetic.

Go. Just go.

Or is that making too much of a fuss?

Be cool. How?

I don't know how long I sat there.

Eventually I peered into the rearview mirror. My reflection peered back.

I look terrible. Better go and bathe my eyes.

Pull yourself together. Play it cool. Pretend you don't care. Don't make a big deal out of it.

I got out of the car, and went back down to the house. David was just waking up.

"Where'd you go?"

"Nowhere. I couldn't sleep so I went out to get some fresh air."

"Did you see the dog?"

"No."

"I wonder where she is. I'd better go and look for her."

"She'll come back."

"She's never been gone this long before."

He got out of bed, dressed, and without another word, went outside.

To hell with the dog. What about me?

He came back twenty minutes later, alone.

"No sign?" I said.

"No."

"I'm sure she's fine."

He shook his head. I kissed him.

"You're going to be a real worrywart when you're a dad," I said.

He nodded.

When you're a dad, and I'm a mother.

The thought brought a longing so intense I nearly cried out.

Later. "I wonder where the dog is," he said.

FORGET THE DOG.

Later. The dog was back. We were sitting outside on the deck.

"You'll have to make yourself scarce tomorrow night, Kitten."

"Can't you just tell Maria I'm here?"

"No."

Silence.

"If I go and stay in a hotel, will you come and stay with me?"

"No."

"Why not?" *Why does my voice have to be so plaintive?*

"It wouldn't be very classy of me, would it?"

And it's classy to throw me out? You invited me here.

Silence.

Why can't he say, "I'm really sorry, Kitten. I know this sucks.

I'll put you up in a hotel, and I'll come and see you on my way home from work. I promise I'll make it up to you."

Why?

Silence.

"When did you know?" I said.

"Maria called yesterday afternoon."

So he knew even before last night.

Why did I change my ticket? Why did I let him talk me into it? Why why why?

Silence.

"Maria's out of town from Tuesday to Sunday; that's why I asked you to stay. I didn't think she'd want to come tomorrow. I know it makes you feel like second fiddle."

You and Maria are supposed to have separated.

You're supposed to be with me.

Silence.

I glanced at his hand. The wedding ring glinted.

"Maybe I should just go back to Europe."

Silence.

"If you go, we'll spend even less time together," he said.

Silence.

My voice is lush with hurt. "When you invited me to stay with you, I thought you were—ready. I didn't realize you were smuggling me in under cover of darkness. That—that it was a secret."

Silence.

Sally's words echoed in my head. "Married men are scum. Creeping furtive lying shits."

Silence.

"Oh, David, I want you to be so proud to be seen with me. Not embarrassed and ashamed."

Stupid bitch, keep your mouth shut.

"I'm not ashamed of you. I'm ashamed of myself," he said, his voice almost a wail.

Silence.

"Come on, Kitten, it's getting cold out here. Let's go make some dinner."

The kitchen was clean. The surfaces were clear of crumbs, no dirty dishes sat on the counter, no clean ones waited to be put away. The only thing out of place was a half-drunk cup of coffee sitting in the sink.

He doesn't drink coffee.

Maria. She was here last night. That's why we couldn't be here. That's why he couldn't stay the night with me.

That's why we were taking stupid risks in San Francisco.

GODDAMN HER.

My hands were hurting. I looked down to see that I was clenching my fists.

"David. When did you last see Maria?"

Hesitation. Then, "Thursday."

Liar. You fucking liar.

But I said nothing.

Later. As we were walking past his bedroom back to the guest room, I said, "You've got a new bed."

"Yeah. Bought it in the fall."

It was a four-poster. How I wanted to be tied to it, spread-eagled. Left to wait and wait. Before being ravished.

"David—" I said, voice tentative.

"Yes, Kitten?"

"Why—why are we sleeping in the guest room?"

You know the answer. Are you bent on getting hurt?

"The sheets aren't clean in the other room," he said.

No. That's not why. It's because that's where you still sleep with Maria.

You've spent more time together during your "separation" than we have in our whole relationship.

As we got into bed, I heard myself saying, "David."

"Yes, Kitten."

"I—" I stopped. "I don't want to have anal sex anymore. I mean it. It hurts too much."

He looked at me. "It's supposed to hurt."

Bullshit. Millions of gay men have anal sex; they don't scream and scream and scream every time they fuck.

But I didn't say that. I said, "Please, David. Please."

A shadow crossed his face. "I'll think about it."

Have I made a mistake?

I fidgeted in the back of the car. *Well, it's done now. I'm leaving. Going back to Europe.*

Wish the driver would shut up. How does my mouth manage to say, "Yes, no, really?" while my mind is churning like this. Just don't cry. Don't cry. Don't let him see.

My face was a grinning rictus.

Somehow I got through the drive to the airport, checked in. But when I got to the departure lounge, memories of happier partings swept over me, and I broke down. I sat, huddled over my bag, oblivious to the stares of the other passengers, unaware of my wet face, my contorted mouth, my swollen eyes.

Again and again, I went over the day before. Again and again,

I saw his wedding ring glinting; I saw the coffee cup in the sink. And fragments of our conversation went around and around in my head. *I want you to be so proud to be seen with me . . . second fiddle . . . I'm ashamed of myself . . . when you're a dad . . . I want you to be so proud . . . so proud . . . so proud . . .*

Why did I have to make such a big deal about it? Why couldn't I have just gone to a hotel? If only I had.

If.

Would it have made a difference? Maybe.

And yet, even then, I still thought everything might work out. I still hoped.

Stupid bitch.

In the evening, we'd made jambalaya together. I'd made a salad. "Do you have a salad bowl?"

"Yes. Should be in that cupboard. It's red."

I couldn't find it. He looked. Nothing. He screwed up his face in puzzlement.

"Maybe Maria took it," he said. "Use this," he said, handing me a mixing bowl.

"Okay, Kitten, I think we're ready to eat," he said. "Let's have a glass of wine."

He reached for a bottle of red. It was half drunk, and had been carelessly recorked.

"We don't buy wine," he said.

We? I wanted to hit him.

"It comes into the house when other people bring it. This one's pretty good."

But how long has it been open?

The jambalaya was spicy and sticky. I took a second helping. But the wine tasted of vinegar. It had obviously been open for weeks. The strange thing was, he didn't seem to notice.

And then, as I was sitting in the airport, I saw. *It's a confidence trick. When he orders such fabulous wine in restaurants—it's just a confidence trick. He's memorized a couple of good labels. That's all. He can't taste it. His know-how is an illusion.*

What else is a confidence trick? His assurances to you?

I shivered, and closed my mind to the questions.

As I walked onto the plane, I wondered what had happened to the leftover jambalaya. I'd wanted to take some for the flight, but I was still looking for it in the fridge when the car came. I couldn't ask David. He'd got up at five, tense and preoccupied, to go to work.

What would life with him really be like?

ZERO

I LOOKED out of the window. Grubby domestic chimneys below. Gray skies above. Bloody London. At least it's not raining.

The waiter rattled in with an enormous trolley elaborately set for two—linen napkins, racks of toast, glasses of orange juice, pots of tea and coffee, jugs of milk and cream, bowls of sugar, dishes of marmalade, and two immense plates capped by faux-silver domes. He wheeled this feast to the foot of the bed, and pulled up two chairs, setting one at each end.

"Thank you," I said, as I signed the check. The waiter leered at me—why? Did he notice that I'm naked under the bathrobe? Or did he spot the riding crop on the desk? The dildo?—then swaggered out of the room. The dark, heavy door clicked shut behind him.

I poured myself a cup of tea and got back into bed.

Waiting. Again.

I hope he gets here soon.

The eggs are going to get cold. He won't like that. Not after a long flight.

Why isn't he here yet? He should be here. The flight landed ages ago. Maybe the traffic is bad. Maybe I should have gone to meet him.

Quit it. I'm not going to fret. Not about where he is. Not about the past. Not about the future. Not going to fret. I'm going to read the paper.

My eyes traveled over headlines, down columns; my hands turned the pages. My mind took no notice. Anxious thoughts chased each other around my skull.

Damn it.

Stop thinking about it.

But I couldn't. My mind insisted on going back through the ten days since I'd left California. The unaccustomed silence. The anxious, gut-wrenching hours of willing the stubborn, silent phone to ring. *What's going on? What's the matter? Why doesn't he call?*

Then: *At last. It's ringing!*

"David?"

"What's up, Kitten?"

His voice sounded dull. Defeated.

"Are you okay?" I said.

"We were seen."

Oh no. NO.

"Nina saw us at the House of Nanking. She told her mother."

I TOLD YOU TO TELL MARIA.

Why did you have to be so stubborn? Why wouldn't you listen? Why why why?

Silence.

"When did you find out?" I said.

"Monday night. I got shat on from a great height." His voice was distorted. Thin.

Monday. The day I left.

"I shamed her in front of her daughter. If I'd told her you were here, then when Nina told her, she could have said, 'I know, David told me.'"

Breathe.

"But she didn't know." His voice cracked. "It was Valentine's Day, Kitten."

Silence.

"Nina won't talk to me."

That's what he cares about. More than he cares about you.

Silence.

"It's harder than I thought, being with two women at once," he said.

You're supposed to be with me. WITH ME.

"That night at the House of Nanking, I felt like a line."

"Like a line?"

"Yeah—you know, what we learned in math: where two planes intersect, they make a line. That evening, two planes of my life collided. I felt like a line." He paused. "I've been wanting to tell you; you're the only person I could say that to, no one else would understand."

Great.

"I feel like you're my drug. I want to be with you so badly that I'm treating other people like shit," he said.

His voice reeked of self-loathing.

"I've broken my promises to her. My wedding vows."

I wanted to shout, "You promised the wrong person!"

But I said nothing.

I looked out at the gray London sky.

I shouldn't have come.

Stop it.

The eggs are getting cold. Wish he'd arrive.

Someone is knocking.

I opened the door.

It's him.

He looked frazzled. Drawn.

"David!"

"What's up, Bitch?" He came into the room, dragging his suitcase behind him.

"I got you some breakfast. Poached eggs. I hope they're not cold. How was the flight?"

"No taxis," he said. "Long line. Took forever."

He glanced at his watch. "What time is your meeting?" I asked.

"Nine thirty. I've got time to fuck you." He shrugged off his coat. "Offer yourself."

I took off the bathrobe, got onto the bed, and held myself open. He stripped, and climbed behind me. He fucked hard, greedily, and fast.

"That's better," he said, a few minutes later. "Now I'll have some breakfast."

I flushed. I'd wanted him to take his time. I felt oddly humiliated.

He put on a bathrobe, looked under both domes, and then sat down in front of the plate of poached eggs. I put my robe back on and went to sit opposite, but he grabbed my wrist.

"No. You sit on the floor," he said.

"No, David."

"Yes, Bitch. And not on the robe, either. I want your pussy on the rug. By my feet."

I swallowed. He stood up slowly, his eyes narrow. "Don't make me tell you again," he said.

I looked at him. He raised an eyebrow. "My bitch is getting fresh," he said. "I'd better remind her what she is."

He pulled me toward him.

"No, David."

"Yes."

I struggled. No use. Suddenly I was across his lap, ass in the air, head dangling.

"I'm going to give you an old-fashioned spanking," he said. I could hear his smile.

He lifted the bathrobe, and ran his hand across my buttocks, stroking, caressing, anticipating.

Then: *wham, smack, wham.* Again. Again. Again.

Stings. It stings.

He slid his fingers between my thighs, and discovered what I already knew.

My pussy was dry.

WHAM, SMACK. He is hitting harder, harder.

I lost count of the blows.

"Now I'm going to eat my breakfast," he said, letting go.

I slid off his knee and onto the floor beside him.

He patted my head. "Good girl," he said. My ass was hot, smarting. The carpet felt scratchy against it.

My pussy was still dry.

He ate in silence, occasionally pausing to feed me with his fingers.

"Open up." I opened my mouth; he inserted a piece of egg on toast. I licked his fingers.

"What are you?" he said.

"Your bitch."

"That's right. You're my bitch and you're sitting at my feet while I eat. It's where you belong."

I shivered, and found myself leaning over to kiss the top of his left foot. The skin was cool. His foot smelled of shoes, and sweat.

He drank his orange juice, then sat back in the chair, glanced at me, glanced at his watch.

"Get on the bed. I'm going to fuck you again."

Rough. Fast. *Damn it, why is he being so quick?*

"I'm going to clean up, then I've got to jump," he said, vanishing into the bathroom.

A few minutes later, he reappeared, clean shaven and dressed in a suit. He kissed me, and smirked. "I should arrange a reception like this in every city I visit," he said, as he went out of the room.

I shuddered, suddenly afraid.

DAMN IT. I KNEW I SHOULDN'T HAVE COME.

Over and over, I hear the voices in my head. His voice, and mine:

"We were seen. I shamed her in front of her daughter."

"I feel like you're my drug. I want to be with you so badly that I'm treating other people like shit."

"I want you to be so proud to be seen with me. Not embarrassed and ashamed."

"I'm going to go. I'll come back when you're ready to be seen with me."

"I felt like a line."

Over and over and over.

Make it stop.

I discovered that I was sitting, naked, on the edge of the bed with my head in my hands. Tears were pouring down my face. My body was shaking with cold.

Pull yourself together. Have a good time with him. That's the most important thing. If you can have a good week together, maybe you can repair the damage.

Must have a good time. Show him a good time. Hide your anxiety. Keep it light.

Maybe if we have fun this week, maybe—

Maybe I can save it.

That night, he took off his belt and beat me with it until I bled. He didn't fold it over into a loop, as he always had before. He beat me so that it coiled around me like a whip.

We'd just come in from dinner. Apart from a pool of light from a lamp on a table by the window, the room was dark. As the door closed behind us, he grabbed me, bending me at the waist, pulling my arms forward so my hands were against the wall. He flipped my skirt up over my back, pulled my underwear down.

He beat me as though he was angry. As though it was all my fault. *Brutality without tenderness.*

My fingernails scraped and scrabbled at the wall as I tried not to scream. *I am not going to scream. I AM NOT GOING TO SCREAM.*

My legs collapsed.

I crumpled at his feet, whimpering. Bleeding.

I still have a row of scars from that night. Along my right hip. A row of commas written into my skin.

Of all the little time we spent together, of the days snatched here and there, the rest of that week in London is the least distinct. Until the end.

On Friday night, thirty-six hours before he was due to leave, we went to the theater. I was already on edge. The week had been tense, violent, without tenderness. I was dazed with shock, too cowed to protest. He had beaten me savagely, again, that after-noon.

The performance was overwhelming. When the end came, when the final, massive explosion left everybody dead, I wept and wept, tears pouring down my face like rain in a monsoon. I found the ticket stub the other day. "Comedy Theatre. Stalls Row D Seat 11. Latecomers not admitted," it said. The play was *Journey's End*.

We emerged into a dim and dirty street. A drunk was pissing against the wall of a nearby cinema, and a couple of teenage thugs ran past us. I felt blank, drained, shell-shocked.

"It's seedy round here," said David.

"Yeah. It's always horrible in this part of town at this time of night. Where would you like to go for dinner?" I said, blowing my nose.

"Let's get a cab back to the hotel. I want to fuck you again. We can order room service."

A taxi, flagged down. His hand, feeling, probing, pinching my naked pussy as we sped past Buckingham Palace to the hotel. Des-ultory conversation about the play. Bright lights in the hotel lobby, reflecting off the mirrors, the marble floor. Waiting for the elevator.

That was when I felt it. Something in his eyes made me afraid. Not a little scared: really afraid.

I swallowed. "Be kind to me, David."

Silence.

Elevator doors opening, closing, opening. Footsteps muffled; eyes hidden in the darkness of the corridor, black walls, black doors. A hand in the small of my back, pushing me forward.

The door, open, closed.

"Get on the bed. Pretty dog. Don't take off your dress."

I knelt. All fours. Back arched. Head up.

He walked around me. He looked as though he were drinking me in. Me in the black dress he had bought me, in stockings and shoes.

He stripped, slowly, deliberately, then climbed up behind me and lifted my skirt, draping it over my back.

Suddenly, I knew what he was going to do. I didn't want it—really didn't want it—and he knew it.

He knew; he knew how to read me; he knew. *I see you. I know who you are, where you are.* But he did it anyway.

"No!" I yelled, "No, David, please!" I shot forward, flattening myself against the bed, and tried to squirm away.

"Yes," he whispered. "If you won't give it to me, I'll take it by force."

He put one hand on my back, the other over my mouth, and rammed his penis into my asshole.

I screamed and bucked and struggled. But I was helpless, and the screams turned to muffled, throaty gasps against his hand.

My body felt like it was being ripped in two.

I was screaming, struggling, trying to bite his hand, trying to make him stop.

I couldn't.

He was right. When you are face down, and someone twice your weight is on top of you, there's nothing you can do.

Eventually, my body went limp. He went on, ramming, shoving, assaulting, splitting me apart.

Suddenly, he pulled out, and in one motion, replaced his cock with the glass dildo.

He stood up.

"Get up and wash me, Bitch. Wash my filthy prick. Then I'm going to fuck your pussy."

I heard him turn on the shower.

I staggered as I got up. My legs wobbled, and I had to grab at the wall to stop myself falling. I moved as though in a dream. Nothing felt real. I was only vaguely aware of my body aching. My mind was numb.

I came into the bathroom. He was already in the shower. As I crossed the floor, the dildo fell out and bounced on the marble floor. He heard the clink.

"Shouldn't you pick that up and put it back in?" he said.

I shook my head. He cocked an eyebrow. I shook my head again, and staggered toward him. He gestured to his cock and held out a piece of soap. I reached out to take it.

But I was beginning to sway. My eyes were filling with blackness. I—

The floor was cold against my cheek.

The floor? Why am I on the floor?

"Are you okay?"

I looked around. David was kneeling beside me, naked and dripping.

"What? What happened?"

"You fainted," he said. "I've never seen anyone faint before."

I glanced at him.

"Come on," he said, putting his hands on my shoulders and helping me to sit. His hands were wet. "Let's get you into bed."

I don't want to move. Not yet.

"In a moment," I said.

He stood, picked up a towel, and began drying himself. "I'm getting cold," he said, laughing.

All of a sudden I found I was crying. Deep, convulsive, wracking sobs.

David looked at me, then turned and left the room.

Eventually, I got to my feet and struggled out of the dress and dropped it into the bathtub. I was still crying—but quiet tears, now. My legs shook when I stood, and I staggered to the sink to wash.

Christ, is that me in the mirror? Is that really me?

I look terrible. My eyes are swollen, my face is streaked, my hair is tangled, my skin is pale. Good lord, I look so thin. And pulped. I have bruises on my breasts and belly, on my thighs and buttocks, on my arms. And what is that expression? Is it fear?

I look as though I've been stripped of emotional protection. There's something naked about my face.

I look broken.

I wobbled to the door, and stumbled back into the bedroom.

David was lying in bed, reading a novel. He glanced at me as I came around the corner from the bathroom, then returned to his book. He didn't put it down.

I got into bed beside him.

He took no notice.

I was shaking. I was crying, crying, crying, shuddering, crying.

David went on reading.

"Please," I said.

He looked over at me, cocked an eyebrow.

"David, please. Put down that book and hold me. Please."

He gazed at me, almost as if he had never seen me before. Then, with a small sigh, he marked his place in the book, and put it down. He shifted his body to make room for me, but he didn't take me in his arms.

I was weeping into his shoulder. I was shivering against him.

He did not try to comfort me. He said nothing. He did not stroke my hair, or try to dry my eyes.

After a few minutes, he pushed me away, and picked up his book again.

"Please. David. Please. Put out the light. Hold me. Please." My voice was pleading, miserable.

He looked over at me, considering.

Then he shrugged, closed the book, and put out the light.

"Good night, David."

"Good night, Kitten."

I went to curl up against him, to rest my head on the crook of his shoulder, but he rolled onto his side, turning his back to me. A few minutes later, he was snoring.

I was still awake, my face wet with tears, when the birds began to sing.

I slipped out of bed. He slept on. When I stood up I nearly fell: my legs were wobbly and my body ached and I was weak with hunger. I walked slowly, awkwardly. My eyes hurt. I dressed in the bathroom, and splashed cold water on my face.

Outside, the air was cool. An early cherry tree was in blossom, and a robin was singing in its branches, serenading the world.

The beauty of the morning was too much, the sadness and hurt in my body too great, and I started to weep as I walked. I didn't care who saw.

I found a café on a small back alley, not far from the hotel. I bought some coffee, and ate a sort of fruit tart, which I normally would have considered a decadent breakfast; but I hardly noticed what went into my mouth. I was too busy, too absorbed in the evening before.

Again and again I heard him say, "If you won't give it to me, I'll take it by force."

Take it by force. Take it by force. The words echoed.

So did other fragments, things we'd spoken of months before. "What are your fantasies, David? I'm living one of mine. . . . You own something completely when you can throw it away . . . throw it away. . . . She knows you're property. . . . Sometimes you have to be cruel to be sexy . . . property . . . throw it away . . ."

And I was remembering things I had tried not to see, not to think of. Little lies, "I'm sorry, my car only has two seats"; Maria's coffee cup in the kitchen sink; wine that tasted of vinegar.

I was afraid.

Afraid that those fabulous, shimmering dreams he had dreamt for me—for us—were about to shatter.

I sat for ages, oblivious to the world, lost inside my skull.

When I got back to the hotel, David was just waking. "What's up, Kitten?" he said. He looked relaxed and refreshed.

"I brought you some breakfast. And a newspaper."

"Oh, thanks. You have the newspaper. I want to finish this book. Get in," he said, gesturing to the bed.